Chance

By

Patrick Lindsay

Copyright 2018

... Holding the Winchester in my right hand, I sprinted for the two large boulders in front of me. I caught a blur of movement in front as I dove the last few yards for the cover of the rocks. Bullets whined above my head. I squirmed along the base of the boulders to the edge, put the barrel of the Winchester around the corner and fired a couple shots in their direction, just to keep them honest.

I studied the area around me. Nothing was moving out there at the moment. I looked for any place they could be hiding, other than behind the rocks, but saw nothing else to give them cover. Far to my right, partially hidden in a small stand of trees, were three ponies. Well, at least I had a pretty good idea of how many of them I was dealing with.

I assessed my situation. Between the two boulders was a crevice I could use to shield the barrel of the Winchester. It gave me a limited view to my front and to my right. I felt pretty confident I could keep them at bay in that direction, assuming there were no more than two or three of them. To my left it was a little more worrisome. The angle of the boulders gave me less vision to that side. It was possible they could flank me if I wasn't careful. I took a small swig of water and kept a watch to my front, and as best I could, to the left flank. Time dragged by. They didn't seem to be in a hurry. The sun rose overhead and I took off coat. I had enough water to last me for a couple days, but I was more concerned about what would happen if I was still here when evening fell. I checked to my front one more time then crawled over to look at my left flank. Had I seen movement out there or was it my imagination?

Chapter One

The journey by rail had been uneventful so far. The train had left the station at Wyandotte, Kansas only about 30 minutes ago. The flat grasslands spread out to the horizon from my seat at the window and I had faint memories of having travelled this way before, down the Santa Fe Trail with my parents when I was just a little boy. They had hoped for a fresh start and a good life in the western lands. My father had named me Chance, because he believed every man had a chance in this country if he worked hard and put his mind to it. He and my mother had come from Ireland, looking for that chance for themselves and their children. Our surname was O'Reilly, but the army had somehow shortened that to Reilly, and that's the name I went by now.

Just a week ago I had been in New York, living a life that wasn't entirely of my own choosing, knowing it was up to me to make changes if I wanted a life I could be proud of. My life in the West seemed a long time ago, but returning to it now made sense to me. If anybody could use a fresh start and some better days ahead, it was me. As the miles rolled by, I turned and stared out the window again, seeing the occasional small herd of buffalo feeding on the grass. They were much less plentiful than I remembered.

The motion of the train and the hot sun through the window made me sleepy. The train was only half full, with no one sitting next to me or across from me. I scooted a little to the side on the bench and rested my head on my coat, up against the window. Somewhere along the way I drifted off to sleep.

I woke up when the train jolted me and a blast of steam escaped the engine. I looked out the window and saw that we had stopped at a siding to take on additional wood. There were just a few nondescript buildings around the railroad siding, and few signs of life. We stayed just long enough to load up a flatcar with the split logs, and then sparks flew from the engine as we gradually picked up speed and pulled away. I looked out at the late afternoon sun and thought about the life I'd just left behind.

I was alone in this world and that thought weighed heavily on me at times. I'd had an aunt and uncle in New York City who had been kind to me and taken me in after I'd lost my parents. The four of them had come together to their new country, but while my parents had dreamed of moving west, my aunt and uncle were content to stay in the east. I'd come back to them at thirteen years of age, and I know I was a handful. There were many ways for an orphaned Irish boy could get into trouble in the early 1860's in New York City, and I'd found several of them.

They'd insisted I get more schooling and that was good for me. It was the things outside the schoolroom that had caused me trouble. My uncle had worked at the docks and I'd helped him from time to time, and it was a rough and tumble life. I had spent a lot of time with the other Irish boys in the neighborhood as well, and we spent more time fighting than anything else. We organized into neighborhood gangs. My uncle had finally taken me aside and told me that if I got into trouble with the law, I didn't have a place under his roof any more. I solved the problem in 1864 at age sixteen by lying about my age and enlisting in the Union Army.

The army was hungry for new troops and we didn't spent much time in training. We joined Warren's V Corps as the Army of the Potomac tried to advance through Northern Virginia, and we found that the rebels had plenty of fight left in them. I was fortunate to be at the rear for the first few actions we encountered, but then found myself in the thick of the fight for Petersburg in June of 1864. On the morning of June 18th we were ordered forward as a part of a general assault on the Confederate troops. After an initial breakthrough, we were scrambling up a hill toward a second Confederate position when I felt a wicked blow in the left thigh and went down. The bullet passed through cleanly but did a lot of damage. Unlike so many others, my leg was saved, but I finished the war with the troops guarding Washington D.C. On rainy days, I still had a slight limp to remind me of my time in the army.

I came back to the present as the train lurched and continued on to the west, with the shadows lengthening when I glanced out the windows. The conductor came by and I asked him when the next stop would be. "Ellis, Kansas, tomorrow morning," he said, barely glancing at me as he went by. I dug into my knapsack for a little beef jerky and settled in for another night on a train. I watched out the window as the darkness deepened and eventually drifted off to sleep.

Morning found little change in the scenery. We pulled into the station at Ellis and disembarked to stretch our legs. A boarding house served breakfast, which turned out to be a bowl of beef and beans. I wasn't sure how well the bowl had been washed, but I wasn't going to complain. I went out back to walk around as much as I could before the train pulled away again. There was just a small collection of weathered clapboard buildings and it took only a few minutes to make a complete lap around them. I came back to the train, where the conductor told me we would arrive in Denver by evening. From there I planned to buy a horse and ride down to the area around Cimarron, New Mexico. It was there I had lived as a boy and hoped to live again.

I dozed again as the train moved west and north. I awoke from time to time and saw more hilly terrain, and finally, mountains pushing up toward the sky, off in the distance. The window of the train felt cooler to my touch. As we moved closer to Denver, I thought about the years since the war and my decision to come west.

When I returned to New York after the war, I found that my uncle had been unable to continue working at the docks. He had become a shopkeeper with the help of a group called the Tammany Society, or sometimes they were called Tammany Hall. I found that they had lent him the money to begin his business, and it was patronized and supported by fellow Irish immigrants. I helped him in his shop, and through his contacts, also found some work at the docks. The population of New York had swollen since the end of the war, and conditions were bad in much of the Five Points area where we lived. I got the impression that my aunt and uncle were very dependent on other Irish immigrants, of which there were a great many ever since the time when we had arrived in the 1840's. The Tammany Society sometimes brought food to help us out, and I was fortunate enough to live in a room above the shop.

I drifted without a lot of direction in those days, dividing my time between the shop and the docks, earning enough to feed myself and help my aunt and uncle, but no more. After a few years, I came to make the acquaintance of someone I knew only as The Boss. Later I came to know him as Boss Tweed. He was a member of the New York Senate when I met him, and I found that it was worth good money to me to do his bidding. My aunt and uncle cautioned me against being too closely associated with him, but the money and the circles he seemed to move in were intoxicating to me. By the spring of 1871, The Boss arranged for me to get a job as a bellhop at the Metropolitan Hotel.

The Metropolitan site on 51st Street was close enough for me to reach by foot every day, but in walking those few blocks, I left one world and entered another. The plate glass mirrors were said to the largest in the world; the patrons were wealthy and beautifully dressed. Guests came from foreign countries as far away as Japan. When I carried my first set of bags to one of the rooms, I found that they were steam heated—a luxury I had never heard of. I was tipped well by the guests and I began to save a little money for the first time in my life. I knew I had the job only because I had the approval of Boss Tweed. When he asked me to hang out at the voting sites on Election Day with others and lean on a few folks to vote the way The Boss wanted, or when he asked to deliver envelopes to certain politicians or businessmen, no questions asked, who was I to question him? There were whispers about carpenters and other workmen close to The Boss becoming wealthy by doing a little work on the County Courthouse and other government projects, but I was benefitting also, and I chose to look the other way.

Two things happened to change the life I had settled into. First, newspaper articles began to appear, charging that The Boss had been at the center of a large amount of corruption, overcharging for building projects, exchanging jobs for favors and selling privileges. In spite of his role in founding and supporting charities, orphanages, and other public works, opinion began to turn against him, and eventually he was investigated and prosecuted. After making bail on a conviction, he was eventually sent to jail for a year, then returned to jail later, unable to make bail this time. My life began to unravel, and now I understood why my uncle wanted me to keep more distance from him.

The second event that changed my life was my uncle's declining health. He had known only a hard life of eighteen and twenty hour work days in the bad sections of Dublin and New York, and it took its toll. His health continued to decline until the spring of 1876, when he passed away. My aunt decided to sell the shop and return to her mother and sister in Ireland. I saw her off on the ship she took home, and then gathered up my few belongings and the little money I had saved and boarded a train headed west. Age twenty-eight seemed as good a time as any to start afresh.

The train whistle sounded as we crossed Cherry Creek and we made our arrival in Denver, now the capital city of the new state of Colorado. The railroads and recent silver strikes had created a boom town in Denver. Besides the usual saloons, hotels, and mining supply stores, I saw a number of restaurants and even a couple of theaters. The buildings seemed a lot newer than those in New York, and the air was crisp and clean, but I had no desire to live in a city again. I disembarked with my knapsack, breathed in deeply and started down the street in search of a place to stay for the night.

Chapter Two

I came down the stairs at Parker's Boarding House the next morning and found the owner, who asked to be called only Ma, serving up breakfast to three other boarders. I ate, paid her for the food and lodging, and asked where I could buy a horse, guns and supplies. She merely pointed down the street and told me I could find all three I if went out, turned right and kept walking. I walked a mile or so until I came to the livery stables, walked in and asked about horses for sale.

It had been a while since I'd ridden a horse, but I had in mind a horse with plenty of endurance for herding cattle. He also needed to be nimble enough to take me through a mountain pass if needed. A little speed would come in handy too. The livery stable owner digested this information and watched the horses milling around in the corral. He rolled the tobacco chew in his mouth, turned around and spit. "It'll cost you." I shrugged and watched as he threw a noose over a sorrel gelding, maybe fifteen hands, and brought him over. We put a saddle and bridle on the sorrel and the proprietor handed me the reins. I climbed on.

The sorrel crow-hopped a couple times at the unfamiliar rider, then settled down to a steady gait around the corral. I got down, looked him over for a while, checked his feet and his teeth, then turned around and offered $150. The man snorted and spit again. "Two hunnerd." We argued back and forth for a while. Eventually, I walked away with the horse, a bridle, saddle and blanket for $190. I named the horse Archie, for no particular reason.

I climbed on Archie and headed back down the street toward the boarding house. I stopped in front of a store with a sign proclaiming firearms for sale and walked inside. A middle aged gentleman with a pair of glasses perched on the end of his nose walked over and held out his hand.

"Tom," he said. "Chance," I told him. We shook hands. "What can I do for you, Chance?"

"I need a rifle and a pistol, with ammunition for both," I told him. He led me to a display in the back of the store and took down three rifles from the shelves, laying them down on a countertop. He picked up the first.

"Spencer Carbine," he said, handing it to me. "Light, fast, and easy to carry in the saddle. Are you passing through any Injun territory?" I told him I was riding down through southern Colorado to New

Mexico and he took the rifle back. "You'll need something more rapid-fire."

He handed me the second rifle. "Henry," he said. "It's accurate and can fire twice as many per minute as the Spencer." I hefted the rifle to my shoulder and sighted down the barrel. "It's heavy," I observed, and looked at the last rifle on the countertop. He handed me the last one. "Winchester 1873 model," he said. Lever action, rapid fire, and lighter than the Henry. I sell more of these than anything else." I lifted the rifle to test the weight and feel of it, and sighted down the barrel. "I'll take it."

Tom took the Winchester from me and set it down near the register. He moved down toward a display of revolvers and began to set some out on the countertop. "That's OK, I told him. Just give me the 1873 Colt revolver." Tom glanced back and grinned slightly. "The Peacemaker?" I nodded. He carried the revolver to the register and set out ammunition, then scratched some numbers on a piece of paper. "$38 altogether," he said. I winced. The $275 I'd brought with me from New York was disappearing fast. "Will you throw in a holster?" He thought for a second, then nodded and laid a holster on top. I counted out some gold coins, took my purchases outside, strapped on the Colt revolver and loaded the rest of my purchases in the saddlebags.

My last stop in Denver would have to be the general store. I went in to buy some food, mainly beans and beef jerky, along with a cooking pot and a few other items. At the last minute I realized I had nothing to sleep on, so I bought a bedroll and blanket. I paid for my items, and then asked the shopkeeper about a trail south into New Mexico. He tore off a thick piece of wrapping paper, sketched out a route on it, and handed it to me. "Watch yore scalp," he said. "Those Apaches might not take kindly to you passin' through. You lookin' for gold?"

That got my attention. "Gold?" He turned around and started stacking some shirts on a shelf. "Yep. Prospector by the name of John somebody came through here a few weeks ago with some gold ore. Said it came from the Sangre de Cristo Mountains down there. West of where you're goin' through. Wouldn't say nothin' else about it."

Well, that gave a man something to think about. That and I had to keep an eye peeled for the Jicarilla Apaches I knew were there along my travel route. I looked at the paper and saw that he had marked out mountain ranges, rivers, and a trail to the south. I tucked it inside my shirt, went out, mounted on Archie, and turned him south toward my destination. I checked my map while riding out of town. The first stop that night, I hoped, would be the town of Pueblo. Archie seemed eager to keep moving at a steady pace, so I pushed on throughout the day, passing through some small rocky hills and scraggly pine trees. The broken clouds gave me a break from the sun and made it a pleasant ride. I stopped occasionally to give Archie some water and a little rest. When I saw Pueblo lying south of me in the distance, I pulled off the trail and made camp for the night.

Morning found me headed south again, and the storekeeper's question about hunting for gold in the Sangre de Cristo Mountains returned to my mind. I could see some peaks of the eastern range to my west as I rode, and found that I more and more wanted to look around. I planned to reach the northern route of the Santa Fe Trail before dark. By mid-morning, I decided I had time to ride over and explore a bit in the mountains. I nudged Archie over onto a faint trail I saw reaching out toward the snow-capped peaks.

As we covered a few miles, the elevation began to climb and I found myself passing through increasingly thick stands of juniper, spruce and aspen trees. Archie began to labor a little bit as we climbed, and I pulled over now and then to give him a breather. I saw a few tracks of black bears and mountain lions, so I kept a sharp eye out as we passed through. Mostly though, I remembered the shopkeeper's warning about hostile bands of Jicarilla Apaches. We forded a few rushing streams and continued to climb. After another hour, we reached a fairly high hill with a good view toward the east. I was mindful not to outline myself against the sky, so I pulled Archie back under a thick stand of trees and took stock of what I saw around me.

I thought of what I knew about mining in the wilderness. One way it was done was to pan the mountain streams. You just sifted the runoff from areas you hoped were laden with gold ore and looked for the gold flakes in the pan. The other way I knew of was more physically demanding. You looked for the veins of gold ore on the walls of crevices or caves on the sides of the mountains or rock formations, and then worked them with a pickaxe. Seeing the natural caves and rocky walls around me, I figured that was the more likely way to do it here. I wasn't allergic to hard work, so that part didn't bother me. The problem was more likely to be about refining the ore you accumulated. With a horse and maybe one or two pack animals, you might not have the ability to pack enough ore out of here with one or two trips. Making multiple trips would attract a lot of attention, and there was still the problem with the Apaches.

I heard the sound of a small rock falling down the hill and froze where I stood, listening and looking off to my left. I heard very little, but saw some movement through the trees. I moved Archie back into deeper cover with me, and then put my hand over his muzzle to help deaden any sound he might make. In another minute, I saw a small band of Apache warriors walking single file and leading their horses along a narrow trail on the steep hillside below me. I didn't move a muscle and had to remind myself to breathe as they passed through. I counted six warriors as they filed past. Their eyes were mostly down on the trail before them and they seemed to be looking for signs of any other traffic on the trail. At one point the Apache in the lead raised his hand and they stopped silently behind him for a few minutes, listening and watching. Time crawled while I waited them out. Finally they moved on, thankfully without noticing me in the trees above them. I waited a good half hour after they were out of sight, then mounted up and headed back for the trail toward the Santa Fe Trail. I wondered if they were looking for a gold miner up in those mountains.

Darkness was falling when I reached the Mountain route of the Santa Fe Trail. Luck was with me, because I soon ran across a party of fifteen people or so travelling down the trail. There was strength in numbers, so they invited me to join them for the balance of their trip as far as Cimarron. They would continue on from there, but that was my final destination and I was welcome to join them for that part of the trip. They offered me some dinner and I gladly accepted. I rolled up in my blankets soon after the meal, looking up at the stars and thinking about my last experience on this trail.

We had taken this same northern Mountain Route, planning to stop around the Cimarron area and settle down on a ranch my folks hoped to start there. The southern route was called the Cimarron cutoff and people sometimes mistakenly assumed that route passed through the town of Cimarron. Only the Mountain Route went through the town, after passing over the Raton Pass. The altitude made the route a little more difficult, but it was the best way to avoid Indian attacks in those days.

My mother had developed a fever as we came through the Kansas territory. We were never really sure what brought it on—maybe just the distance and difficulty of the trail wore her down. She didn't improve as the days went by, but there wasn't much choice but to keep moving ahead. Dad made her as comfortable as he could in the wagon and drove on ahead, hoping to reach Cimarron and find a doctor for her there. It wasn't to be. Her fever had steadily worsened, and we buried her just off the trail about a hundred miles from Cimarron. I didn't seem to have any tears left when I thought about it, but I knew that loss would affect me for the rest of my life.

Our party was on the move by daybreak, and we were all anxious to reach town. We pushed steadily along as the morning wore on, stopping only briefly for a little bit of lunch. By early afternoon we saw a small collection of buildings in the distance, and about an hour later pulled into the town of Cimarron. It looked nothing like I remembered, but I considered that I was home. I thought about the small number of gold coins left in my pockets after buying my guns, supplies, and Archie. I figured that first I would find a place to stay, and after that, look for a job of some kind to tide me over while I got my bearings and made plans for my future.

Chapter Three

Cimarron was still an inviting little town, in my opinion, and I was anxious to call it home again. It sat on the bank of the river it was named after, and the Cimarron River fed the Canadian River, which stretched out for nine hundred miles through this part of the country. The town was bigger than I remembered. Wagon trains passing along on the Santa Fe Trail had created a demand for general supplies. To a lesser degree there was a call for mining supplies, and sometimes folks just wanted to stay a night or two in a hotel or eat in a café after spending so much time traveling in a wagon and living along the trail. The population now stood at around 275 people.

I had stayed at the Last Chance hotel last night. The name appealed to me for obvious reasons, though I'd given only my last name when anyone asked. I thought it might be to my advantage if people didn't remember me from my boyhood years here, and it turned out later that I was right. At one dollar per night, I figured I could stay there a couple weeks without working if I didn't eat too much, but then again, eating was one of my favorite things. I walked up and down the main street in the morning sun with the collar of my coat lifted to protect me against the chilly wind. At 6,500 feet elevation, mornings were generally chilly at best, and this late spring morning was no exception.

I took stock of the town as I walked up and down the street. Here and there the doors were boarded up on a place, but in general the town seemed to be thriving. I found about what I expected in terms of establishments—one hotel, one boarding house, two cafes, a general store, a mining supplies store, a few other small businesses, and of course, two saloons. I stopped at one of the cafes for a late breakfast and gave some thought to my money situation. I found that I wanted to look for a short-term job—maybe just for a couple weeks—while I sized up what was happening around town and whether or not I wanted to work at any of the ranches in the general area. My own personal history had made me cautious about who I worked for and associated with.

It seemed to me that a saloon might be a good place to look for some temporary work. They often needed help with tending the bar, cleaning up, or hauling barrels in the back. Turnover in a town like this was an accepted fact. I walked out of the café and back down the street to the sign that had rung a bell when I had walked by earlier—Bart's Saloon. When I lived in the area before, the owner's name was Sam. Why the name was still Bart's Saloon, I had no idea and Sam probably didn't either. I knew that Sam had known my father, but I didn't plan to use that to get some work. In fact, I hoped that Sam wouldn't recognize me. I'd never gone into the saloon with my father, and had only seen Sam a few times in the street some fifteen years ago. Few people even knew my first name in those days. Dad had just called me "Boy-o" in that Irish brogue of his. We'd gone by the true family name of O'Reilly, but I'd found it easier just to leave it as the Army version of the name and generally introduced myself as Reilly.

I climbed the steps to the saloon and passed by a mixed breed hound sunning himself in the dust by the door out front. He managed to wag his tail a couple times without actually lifting his head to greet me. I pushed open the batwing doors, stepped inside and gave myself a few seconds to let my eyes become accustomed the lack of light inside. There were only a few people there, which was to be expected. It wasn't yet noon. A few men sat around a table by one of the windows, playing cards and apparently not drinking just yet. The windows were clean enough to let a small amount of sunlight in, but actually seeing anything through the windows was going to be a different story. One man sat by himself at the bar with a whiskey in front of him. One other man wore a well-used apron and was washing some glasses behind the bar. A toothpick hung from his lips, and he wore a rather sour expression. If memory served, this was Sam. I sat down on a stool at the bar in front of him.

"I'm looking for some work," I told him. "I can serve drinks, sweep up, clean tables, and haul barrels, anything you need." Sam looked up from the glasses and glanced at me briefly. "You got a name?" "Reilly," I told him. The toothpick shifted to the other side of his mouth, but he hadn't blinked yet, so far as I could tell. "How about a first name? You got one of those too?" "Chance." I looked at him for any sign of recognition. There was none. "Ok" he said after he'd looked me over a little. "I'll give you a try. I can't pay you much—only seventy-five cents a day, but I have a spare room where you can sleep for free. Take it or leave it." I reached out and shook his hand. "When can I start?" I asked. He told me he had some things to be moved around in the storeroom and I could start any time. I asked him for a few minutes to check out at the hotel and bring my bag over. I left Archie where he was at the livery stable at the end of town and came back to the saloon to get started.

Several days went by pretty uneventfully as I settled in to a bit of a routine at the saloon. Sam liked to get an early start, or at least it was an early start for a saloon. He came in at about ten o'clock and started cleaning up from the previous day. He kept the glasses washed and the floor swept, which was more than you could say for a lot of similar places. Things stayed pretty slow until the early or mid-afternoon, and he generally gave me a couple hours at around 11:00 to do anything I needed to do.

There were two things in particular I wanted to get done before I left Sam's place and moved on to something more permanent. The first I took care of during those hours off in the mornings. I generally took several empty beer bottles from out back, put them into my knapsack along with my gun and holster, and then went down to get Archie from the livery stable for a ride. Nobody thought twice about seeing me take out my horse for a morning ride. I always rode out to the west and to the cliffs that overlooked the town. A half hour's ride along a lightly used trail into the woods brought me to the same clearing every morning.

I tied Archie to a log several yards away from the clearing, then went to one end of the space and set up my empty beer bottles on another log that ran across the edge for several yards. I stepped off thirty paces across the clearing, then took my pistol from the knapsack and strapped it on. I began to practice drawing and firing the pistol at the beer bottles. When they were all broken, I set up some more. I considered speed to be important but not vital. What I knew was vital was the ability to hit the bottles on the first shot. I kept drawing and firing until I could break six bottles with six bullets. I kept it up for a good half hour. That was my morning routine, and I was becoming accustomed to the weight and feel of the Colt.

My father, being from Ireland, hadn't been much interested in wearing a pistol. He had a shotgun he used for hunting birds and a rifle he carried with him on the ranch. He used the rifle for hunting deer, and protecting himself from bears and mountain lions. He wasn't naïve enough to think he would never have a need for it in dealing with thieves and outlaws, but he hoped he wouldn't. He considered it part of my education, though, to know how to use a pistol, so he'd bought me one and made sure I practiced with it. "Boy-o," he would say, "it seems to me that the most important thing is to hit what you're aiming at. And never draw that gun against another man unless your life depends on it. You don't want a reputation as a gunman. That just brings around another gunmen looking to test himself against you. Get familiar with that gun, draw it smoothly and hit what you're aiming at. No more, no less."

I scraped together the broken bottle remains and buried them, then walked back over to where I'd left Archie. He seemed to have gotten used to this morning routine and was grazing quietly when I came over. He nuzzled me for the half an apple he knew I'd be carrying. I gave it to him and stroked his neck while I thought a bit more about my dad and the ranch we'd established up here. I found it hard to believe that was now twenty years ago.

It was just the two of us when we arrived in Cimarron. The area was settled pretty sparsely back in 1856, so we had just homesteaded several hundred acres several miles to the north of where I was now standing. Dad was from the old country and a little suspicious of how he would be treated as a foreigner. As it turned out, the things we were doing would have allowed us to make a claim to the land just a few years later. The Homestead Act was passed in 1862, at which point we would have lived on the land for more than five years, worked the land, and made improvements to it. All dad would have needed to do at that point would have been to file a claim for the land with the government. It didn't work out that way for us.

I was too little to be of much help at first, but I rode with him when he went out to check the cattle and work the fences. As I got a little older I could help him drive the cattle from the upper pastures to the lower pastures when winter began to set in, and I could haul feed to them and even work a few fence repairs. When Dad needed help to drive some cattle to market or do some of the heavier work, he could generally find someone down at Bart's saloon with time on his hands and the need for a little money. I also remembered a neighboring rancher who had helped him on a few occasions, but couldn't bring that name to mind now.

Several years had passed in this fashion, and it was a good life. I suppose it had been exactly what my parents had in mind when we came to this country. We had some prime property backed up to the river on one side, with lush lower pastures, and in the summer we could drive the cattle to the high pastures, up against the mountains. A stream cut through the upper pastures to give them water, and the cattle had access to the river in the lower pastures. Dad saved some money, and the rough cabin we'd started out with when we'd first arrived became a pretty nice ranch house with a barn and corral.

It was the summer I'd turned thirteen that I first realized trouble might be coming. Three brothers had come to the ranch and talked to Dad. I knew enough to know they were asking Dad to sell the ranch to them, and to know that he'd refused. They'd become louder and more insistent, and Dad had responded in the same way. Their name I remembered: Carson. The one who did most of the talking was Jack Carson. I never did catch the names of the other two brothers. A couple weeks later they rode back up to the house, and Dad met them in the yard carrying his shotgun. He told them to leave the property and not come back. They'd eyed the shotgun for a moment, and then they rode away. We'd hoped that was the end of it.

A few weeks later Dad had ridden out to check the cattle in the high pasture. He'd left me back at the ranch house to do some work. Night fell without him returning. I'd spent the night tossing and turning and checking out the window. At daybreak I rode out to the upper pasture and looked around without finding him. I spent several hours covering and recovering the same ground, calling out his name. By noon I knew I needed help and rode into town. The sheriff and four others rode back with me to the high pasture and spread out to look for tracks. Near the western edge of the pasture they found some recent tracks leading into a stand of trees. They followed the tracks for a few minutes until they emerged at the edge of a cliff. The tracks stopped there. When they looked over the edge of the cliff, they saw Dad lying on the rocks several hundred feet below. His horse was nowhere to be found.

The sheriff had eventually ruled it an accident. They speculated that Dad's horse might have been frightened by a mountain lion or other animal, thrown him, and bolted. In my mind that never answered the question of what he'd been doing at the edge of a cliff. He'd gone up there to check the cattle and wasn't in the habit of going to look at the sights. The sheriff had nothing else to go on, though, and didn't have the time or inclination to start an investigation. I was obviously too young to stay there on my own. We didn't have a claim to the land, anyway. The Sheriff took me back to the ranch and had me gather up my things. Then he took me into town, where an older couple in Cimarron had taken me in for a few weeks. They asked me about relatives, and I told them about my aunt and uncle in New York. When they had made contact with my aunt and uncle, it was decided that I would go back to live with my relatives. The cattle and horses on the ranch were sold and the money was given to me to take along with me to help cover expenses. Then they sent me east by wagon and train to New York.

Archie's ears came up and he snorted, startling me back to the present. I slid my Winchester out of the scabbard and scanned the area around me. I heard and saw nothing. Eventually Archie relaxed and went back to cropping grass. I mounted and rode back into Cimarron.

That second thing I wanted to get done while working at the saloon had entirely to do with the death of my father. I wondered whether the Carson brothers were still in the area. I was undecided whether to try to follow up on how my father had died. A lot of years had gone by. I also wondered what had happened to our ranch after I came east. We had no legal claim to the land, so I suppose anyone could have moved onto it. I started to ask Sam about it a couple times, but always held back, preferring that for now no one else knew about my past ties to the area.

Afternoons at the saloon saw business slowly picking up. An occasional cowboy or traveler came in for an afternoon beer, and then as the afternoon became evening, the card players began to show up and business picked up at the bar. The orders at the bar were only two things: beer and whiskey. If they ordered anything else, they were out of luck because Sam didn't have anything else. There was a piano in one corner, and an old-timer generally came in around eight to do what passed for piano playing. He kept a tin cup on top of the piano for donations, but it never had much money in it. After I'd heard him play on the first night I knew why. It got busiest between around ten o'clock at night and midnight, and after that Sam closed the place. If anybody objected to that too much, Sam kept a shotgun behind the bar to help convince them.

This evening was going as they generally went. Around ten the place was filling up and business was good. Sam asked me to go the back for more whiskey glasses. As I was coming out of the storeroom with the glasses, I heard somebody yell: "Hey Jack, where you been?" It was a common enough name, but I came slowly back through the hallway and looked out into the saloon. I waited for a few people to move and give me a clear view of the room, then stared through the cigar smoke. It had been several years and I had only been a boy, but there was no mistaking it— those faces were only vaguely familiar, but I felt sure I knew what I was looking at. All three Carson brothers were still here.

Chapter Four

Early morning sunlight began to shine weakly through the window in my back room at the saloon. I laid on my bedroll, stared at the ceiling and thought about what I'd learned last night. The Carson brothers were still in the area, or at least they had been last night. I wasn't sure what I wanted to do about that, if anything. Was it best to let sleeping dogs lie?

I got up and shaved in the sink I had in the corner of my room. When I had finished I stepped back and took stock of myself in the broken piece of mirror I had tacked to the wall. I was in good shape, I knew that. The rough and tumble life in New York and the work at the docks had built solid muscles on me. At six feet tall and 185 pounds, I was bigger than most and had learned how to take care of myself the hard way. I'm Irish, but hadn't inherited the red hair and fair skin of so many countrymen. I had taken after my mother's side of the family, with dark hair and dark complexion. I wasn't sure if you could call me handsome or not. I got my fair share of second looks from the ladies, but I couldn't say they exactly pestered me for attention.

I heard Sam come into the saloon out front, and I decided to ask a few questions. I walked out into the saloon, picked up a broom, and started sweeping. Sam glanced up and nodded, then went back to washing glasses. When I finished sweeping, I walked over and sat down at the bar. Sam looked up, a quizzical expression on his face. We didn't talk much, usually. He leaned forward, elbows on the bar. "What's up?" "I've been thinking about trying to get some work on a cattle ranch somewhere around here. Does that cause any problems for you?" Sam shook his head back and forth. "Naw. There's always someone I can hire temporary, when I need some help. You ever do any ranch work?" I told him I'd done some cowboy work and general ranch work when I was younger. I asked him to fill me in on the possibilities around Cimarron.

Sam came around and sat down on the stool next to me. He thought for a minute, and then shifted the toothpick to the other side of his mouth. I wondered how often he changed out that toothpick. "Only two places I can think of around here that might hire some help. I can only recommend you try one of them." "Tell me about both" I told him. "OK," he said, "the first one is owned by three brothers we had in here last night. Carson brothers. Nice piece of land they have up there, upper and lower pastures, good water on both. I don't know how much ranching they really do. Got a few skinny cows running around up there. Every once in a while they sell a few and ship 'em off. I don't know if they've ever hired a hand, but I can't see they do much work themselves. Maybe they would want to hire somebody to do it for 'em."

I sat and digested what he'd just told me. "OK, I said. How long have they had that place?" Sam squinted out the windows and thought for a second. "Maybe twenty years, give or take a couple". Well, I thought, that answers my question about what became of the old homestead. I became aware that Sam was glancing at me sideways, so I swung back around on the stool to face him. "You're right," I told him. "Doesn't sound very inviting. Tell me about the other place."

Sam walked back around the bar and began wiping down the counter. "Other place belongs to a man named Randolph. Jim Randolph. Lives out there with his daughter, maybe early twenties. Her name is Kate. She comes in town with him for supplies, maybe once a month, but never comes in here. He comes in for a beer when he's here. Their spread is next to the Carson place, been up there since before the Carson's. Not quite as well set up a spread, but he runs it right. They generally have one hand, but I don't know if they've got one right now. Jim ain't getting any younger, though.

Maybe he needs a hand or maybe he'd consider another one. I can introduce you when he comes in next time, if you want."

That name rang a bell with me faintly. I supposed it was the neighbor who used to come over and help out Dad from time to time. I seemed to remember a wife as well as a little girl, but Sam hadn't mentioned the wife. I looked up and nodded. "Sure," I said. "Next time he comes in." I got up and grabbed the mop and bucket. Maybe that was the beginning of a plan. I still didn't know what to do or not do about the Carson brothers. Maybe I could ride up to the old place and take a quiet look around.

Around five o'clock that afternoon, with just a few regulars sipping beer at the bar, the doors swung open and an older gentleman wearing a tin star came in. He sat down at a table, and Sam suggested I take a whiskey over and introduce myself. I placed the whiskey at the table and asked if I could join him for a moment. He nodded at the empty chair and held out his hand. "George Stanton," he said. I shook his hand and sat down. He wasn't the same sheriff who'd been here when I was a boy. "Reilly" I told him. "Chance Reilly". He nodded again. "Been here long?" I told him I'd been in town only a few days, but was hoping to stick around. We made small talk for a few minutes while he finished the whiskey, then he moved on.

I walked back to the bar and glanced at Sam. "Always good to meet the sheriff when you're not in any trouble," he said with a grin. "George mostly wants a quiet town. He's honest and he'll do his job, but he doesn't want trouble. He'd rather have it quiet and peaceful than anything else. Won't hurt you any to know that." I nodded and wondered, not for the first time, if Sam remembered more about me than he let on. He was a hard one to read.

Morning came, and after the usual morning chores at the saloon, I decided it was time to do what I'd been putting off—I would ride out to the old ranch and look around. I dug around in my knapsack and found the old pair of binoculars I'd had since I was a kid, slipped them under my jacket and walked down to the livery. I mounted Archie and headed out to the north of town. We began to climb higher, and I buttoned up my jacket against the chill. The stands of pines and firs thickened, and I became more aware of sounds of the wilderness—the chirping of the birds, a mountain stream not too far off, and the occasional rustling of squirrels and other small animals in the underbrush. It had been many years, but there was still a familiarity to the trail I was on. When I thought I might be approaching the ranch house, I swung off the narrow trail I was on and looped around to the west. There had been a ridge atop the fences separating our spread from the neighbors to that side, and I had it in mind to ride up to that ridge and look things over with my binoculars. The trees and underbrush began to thicken as we moved on, but I could see the ridge ahead and above me. I slowed the pace and pushed forward steadily.

I reached the base of the ridge and began to climb, using the trees for cover and keeping the noise to a minimum. After about ten minutes of steady climbing, we crested the ridge. I tied Archie in a stand of pine trees, walked back and found myself a perch behind a couple of boulders and under some trees. I settled down to watch what was happening at the old homestead.

Somebody was at home in the ranch house, because I could see a bit of smoke climbing out of the chimney. There were a few horses in the corral, but not many. The ones I could see probably belonged to the Carson brothers. If they had any hands working stock on the ranch, it didn't seem like there were enough horses there to get the job done. I swung the glasses over to the barn, and saw no activity there. I moved on to what appeared to be a bunkhouse, which was an addition they'd made since the days Dad and I had lived there. I studied it carefully. It didn't appear to be in use. There was no smoke coming from the chimney, and the doors and windows were all closed up tight. There was a hitching rail in front, but no horses were there and I couldn't see any hoof prints on the ground from recent usage. I lifted my gaze to the lower pasture and see only a few head of cattle. I knew that pasture could support a couple hundred head, and it was too early in the year to have taken any to the upper pasture. It seemed strangely deserted.

The front door of the ranch house swung open and I swung the glasses back in that direction. Two men emerged from the house. I recognized the taller one from the saloon the other night—Jack Carson. The other man had to be one of his brothers, but I didn't know the other names. They walked to the corral where each saddled a horse and rode out in the general direction of Cimarron. I looked back toward the ranch house, and saw there was no more smoke coming from the chimney. I toyed with the idea of going down for a closer look, but decided it wasn't worth it if the third brother was still around somewhere. There was still one thing I wanted to do before leaving, though. I stayed where I was for another ten minutes or so before moving out.

I went back to Archie, mounted up, and worked down off the ridge, still keeping to the west of the ranch. I worked my way through the trees to the west of the lower pasture, and then began to climb toward the high pasture, keeping alert for any sign of the other brother or anybody else I wasn't expecting. When I topped a rise now and then, I took out the binoculars to make sure my back trail was clear. I stayed in the trees to the west of the high pasture and stopped Archie at the edge of some trees at the base of a rocky cliff. I took my Winchester out of the saddle bags and scrambled up along the rocks and boulders until I found what I was looking for. There was a small natural cave tucked behind some boulders up there. Dad and I had come across it years before, and he'd brought a few supplies up here in case either of us ever needed shelter and couldn't make it home.

I propped the Winchester against a couple boulders and drew my pistol as I edged up to the cave. I moved quickly into the entrance, stepped inside, and then drew up against the wall as I let my eyes adjust to the light. I could see no sign of any recent use. The blankets we'd left up there were rotting and moldy at this point. I dragged them out and buried them in the woods a couple hundred yards away. I returned and looked around. There were a couple pots and pans we'd left in there that still looked usable. There was an old Henry rifle that Dad had left up there along with some ammunition, but I didn't figure the ammunition was still good. I pushed it off to the corner of the cave. After looking around for a few more minutes, I left the cave, mounted up on Archie, and headed back to Cimarron.

The sun was up high overhead by the time I reached town. I stabled Archie and had my coat over my shoulder by the time I reached the saloon. It was a few minutes past my usual one o'clock afternoon start, but Sam was easy about such things. He was talking to a tall, rangy, iron-haired gentleman I hadn't seen before. Sam waved me over when I walked in. "Chance, this is Jim Randolph. I was just talking about you." He got up from the table to give me his seat and walked away as I shook hands with Randolph.

He looked me over with curiosity. "Sam says you might be looking for some ranch hand work?" I nodded. "That's what I would like to do." He took a pull from his beer, and then looked up at me. "But Sam says you came here from New York. You got any experience on a ranch?" "I grew up just north of here," I said evasively. "I grew up herding cows, working fence lines, doing anything you need me to do. Anything I'm out of practice doing, I promise I can pick it right back up. I'm a hard worker. Just ask Sam." He seemed to stare at me for a long time, and then a small smile played around his lips for a second. "I already asked Sam. OK, I think you'll do. A dollar a day and you can bunk in at the bunkhouse, meals at the house with me and my daughter. Pay for your own ammunition, and if you bring a little deer or elk meat for the dinner table every now and then, that would be nice. Take it or leave it."

I stood up and shook his hand. "I'll make a good hand for you." He nodded. "You can come out to the ranch on Monday and get started." I trailed along after him out the doors of the saloon. He gathered the reins of his horse and mounted up. He looked down at me, that same small smile on his mouth. "Took me a minute to make the connection," he said. "You shortened up the last name, that was part of it. The first name didn't ring a bell at all. Your dad just used to call you 'Boy-O', best as I can recall. Your dad was a good man." He turned and rode down the street and out of town. I stared after him and wondered if he would keep it to himself.

I worked one more day for Sam, helping him lay in some supplies and clearing out the back room. That left me with a few days before I started work at the Randolph ranch the next Monday. On that Friday morning, I decided there was one more thing I would do before then. I rolled out in the morning and walked down to the general store. I bought a bedroll, some blankets, an axe, and several cans of beans. In addition, I bought ammunition for the Henry rifle up there in the cave, and got more ammunition for my own guns. The shopkeeper looked over my purchases and gave me a questioning glance. "Goin' on a trip?" he asked. I shrugged and discouraged further conversation by saying "No, just getting some supplies." He nodded and minded his own business after that.

I rode back up to the cave above the ranch, covering over my trail now and then as I went and keeping an eye out for any of the Carson brothers. When I reached the cave I gathered up the usable things I found there – the pots and pan, an old coffee pot and a broom. I put the blankets inside the bedroll and put them on top of some rocks, off the ground where I hoped it would stay dry. Likewise, I put the Henry rifle and ammunition, as well as the extra ammunition for my guns on a natural shelf at the back of the cave. If took out my binoculars and left them there also. If I needed them for the ranch work, maybe Jim would have an old spyglass or something. I came out and brushed away any footprints or other sign of my entry with a branch I found lying on the ground.

I went outside and gathered up some wood and kindling. What I found was a little wet, but it could dry out inside the cave. Finally, I went back to Archie and took an old knapsack out of the saddle bags. I had a couple changes of clothes inside. I left the knapsack back in a corner of the cave.

On an impulse, I climbed a little farther up the slope and ducked through a notch in the rock formation above me. Coming out on the other side, I looked down on what I knew must be the Randolph ranch below me. I could see the usual collection of buildings— ranch house, barn, bunkhouse and corral. A little smoke lifted from the chimney at the ranch house. I could see no sign of activity at the bunkhouse. I slid back through the notch in the rocks, mounted Archie, and started back toward Cimarron. I hoped I would never need the items I'd left up here, but life had taught me to prepare for the unexpected and watch your back. Being careful was a good thing.

Chapter Five

I stopped off at the saloon before leaving Monday morning. I thanked Sam for the work he'd offered me and also for putting in the good word with Jim Randolph. "You never know," I told him, "if I don't like it there, I might be back and ask for my old spot." "You'll like it there," he said as he wiped down the counter. "You think ranch work will suit me?" I asked. "Probably" he said as he picked up a box and headed toward the back room. He pushed open the door with his foot and turned around briefly. "Plus, there's Kate." He chuckled and went into the back room, closing the door behind him.

Now what was that supposed to mean? I shook my head, went outside, mounted up on Archie and cantered out of town. I knew the Randolph spread was due west of the old place where I'd lived as a kid, so I took the same trail for several miles. When I was close to getting on to the Carson property, I took a trail to my left and followed it for another mile or two. I saw a hand-lettered wooden sign proclaiming the entrance to the Randolph ranch, and followed the trail on in.

I could see Jim Randolph in the corral, talking to a red-haired man and pointing occasionally to the pasture and mountains beyond. The other man was nodding without much enthusiasm, it seemed to me. I rode up, dismounted, and tied Archie to the top rail of the corral. Randolph walked over, hand extended. "Chance," he said simply. "I'm glad you're here." I shook his head and glanced toward the other man, who was introduced to me simply as Red. I shook his hand also, taking in a rather sour expression and overly forceful handshake. I guessed him to be about twelve to fifteen years older than me, a couple inches taller, but thinner. He had a narrow-shouldered look about him, and didn't seem to have much to say to me. Jim Randolph patted my shoulder and pointed toward a small building about 50 or 60 feet away. "Bunkhouse over there," he said. "Put your stuff in there and come back. I'll give you a tour of the place and tell you what I have in mind for you."

I took my knapsack, bedroll, rifle and ammunition along with a few other things and carried them over to the bunkhouse. I shoved at the door with my foot and went inside. One glance told me that Red had never been described as a good housekeeper. There were dirty clothes strewn all around, with a couple dirty dishes mixed in. I could see which bunk he'd been using, so I tossed most of the dirty clothes in that direction and threw my bedroll on the other one. My rifle went under the bed. I tossed the knapsack on top of my bedroll and went back outside.

I could see Jim had moved over to the corner of the barn and was talking to Red, who was out of my sight around the barn. I put my hands in my back pockets and walked on up to them. "I'm moved in" I announced as I came up to Jim. He nodded and stepped back, and I could see that he hadn't been talking to Red, after all. There was a young woman standing there, giving a sack to Jim, and my nose told me it was his lunch. I looked back at the woman and swallowed a couple times. She was probably a few years younger than me and a few inches shorter. Long blonde hair and the bluest eyes I could remember seeing. She was beautiful by any definition. "Chance, this is my daughter Kate. Kate, Chance." It occurred to me suddenly that I should take off my hat. I yanked my hands out of my back pockets and swiped my left hand toward my head. I only succeeded in knocking the hat to the ground. I picked it up and extended my right hand awkwardly. "Ma'am". She took my hand and smiled. "Chance," she said. "Welcome." We shook hands and she turned for the house. I turned my hat around in my left hand a few times and glanced over at Randolph. He was staring at the ground and seemed to be smiling at his boots. "Well," he said eventually and pushed past me toward the corral. "Let me give that tour I promised." I jammed my hat back on my head and followed.

The Randolph ranch had a very similar setup to our old family ranch, which shouldn't have been surprising, considering they were side by side, and the geography through the area was pretty consistent. They had an upper and lower pasture, with good water for both, though the lower pasture was a bit smaller than the ranch claimed by the Carson brothers next door. The main difference, as far as I could see, was that the Randolph ranch on the west stopped at a steep set of cliffs leading up into the mountains. It formed a natural barrier on that western side. The lower pasture was fenced on the west, but the high pasture had no need. We worked the western side from lower pasture to upper, then across the northern side, where the grass gave way to scraggly pine trees and ended at the rocky cliff sides that formed the northern edge of the property. Jim explained that they ran about 200 head of cattle.

We came to the eastern property line, bordering the Carson property, and stopped short at a barbed wire fence that ran across the property line up to the point where the steep rise in elevation made it unnecessary to keep the cattle from straying across the line. We reined in and I stared at the barbed wire, trying to remember if it had been there fifteen years ago. Jim followed my glance. "It wasn't there when you and your dad had that ranch," he said. I nodded. He hesitated, seeming to weigh a decision in his mind.

"I've been missing some cows," he said finally. "Just a few, now and then, but it's been pretty steady for several years now. I put the fence in about 5 years ago, and I'm missing fewer than I was before, but I'm still coming up short by a number of cows every year. We make a decent living from the ranch, and we have the beef and Kate's garden for most of our food, but I can't afford to lose them." His gaze wandered to the neighboring pasture across the fence. "I'm not making any accusations I can't prove, and I'm not asking you to take any foolish chances. But if you see something you think I need to know about, I'm hoping you'll tell me." I nodded. "Of course." I dismounted and walked over to a section of the fence that had caught my eye. The strands of wire had been mended, and I could see the newer sections of wire twisted around the old to close up the former break in the wire. I twisted it a little in my hand to see if it looked like the wire had been cut or had simply snapped from the elements and time. I couldn't tell for sure. Jim watched me silently until I walked back to Archie and mounted up. We turned back toward the ranch house.

We rode in silence for a couple minutes until Jim cleared his throated and reined in his horse. "What I told you about the missing cows," he said. I nodded. "I'd appreciate it if you say nothing to Red about it." I looked over at him, but he was looking down toward the lower pasture and didn't meet my eyes. I nodded. "Of course." I turned Archie to continue the ride back to the house, but Jim hadn't moved, and I could see he had something else on his mind. He twisted the reins in his hand for a minute, and then looked over at me. "You would find this out at dinner tonight, anyway. The youngest of the Carson brothers, name of Yates. He comes callin' on Kate every now and then, has dinner with us sometimes. Kate is a little sweet on him." He fell silent for a minute and I waited. "Not much to choose from in such a small town." His voice trailed away, but I could see the worry in his eyes. "Anyway," he said after a minute, "I haven't talked to Kate about it either, because of her seeing Yates sometimes." He gathered up the reins and started back toward the house.

I gave Archie a little slap on the rump and caught up. "I won't say anything either," I told him. He glanced over and nodded. "Where your history around here is concerned, that's between us, as far as I'm concerned," he told me. "A man's history is his own business. You might want to know, though, that I'm not the only one who figured it out." "Sam?" I asked. "Right," he said. "It took him a few days, but he figured it out too. If you need a friend, you can count on Sam. It's a good thing to know." We rode on down to the house and turned the horses in to the corral. Jim nodded toward the bunkhouse. "I'll let you finish getting settled in. We generally eat supper around six o'clock."

When I entered the bunkhouse, Red was laying on the bunk on the far side of the room. He eyed me with no sign of friendliness when I stepped in. I nodded and began unpacking the few items I had. "Where'd you go?" I glanced around and caught his unblinking stare. "Randolph just showed me around the property," I said, turning around and pushing my knapsack under the bunk. When I turned back, he dropped his stare to the Colt I had strapped on my hip. "You any good with that thing?" I shrugged. "I know how to use it." I held his stare until he could see he wouldn't get any more answer than that. Eventually he lay back on the bunk, put his hands behind his head and looked at the ceiling. "He never said anything to me about hiring another hand," he said, almost to himself. I decided the air was better outside, and went over to the corral to brush Archie until the triangle bell on the porch of the ranch house sounded dinner.

As I climbed the steps to the front porch, I noticed a horse tied to the railing. I skirted around to check the brand: CCC. I knew it must be the youngest Carson brother that Jim Randolph had mentioned. I approached the front door, which stood partially open, and raised my hand to knock when Kate saw me. "Chance," she said, "no need to knock when you're coming for supper. Just come on in." She turned toward a young man who was leaning against the wall. He was a few years younger than me, slightly shorter and a little thinner, sandy hair running a little bit long, wearing a slightly hostile expression. "This is Yates Carson," she said. "He's a friend." He shook my hand but said nothing. "You know Red," Kate continued. She took my arm. "Let me give you a tour of the house. It's a short tour." As we passed Yates Carson, I saw that his expression had turned more than a little bit hostile. I have to say I enjoyed that.

We passed a room on our left just as Jim Randolph was coming out of it. "This is Dad's room," she said, pointing. Jim smiled and patted me on the shoulder as we continued on. She pushed open another door. "This is my room." I stood in the doorway and looked in. There was a four poster bed and a dresser, with a vase of fresh wild flowers on the dresser. As I started to turn away, I noticed a couple paintings on the wall. "Oh," I said as I looked at the paintings. "Do you mind if I take a closer look?" She smiled.

"Go ahead." As I walked over to look at them, it seemed to me they were paintings of the high pasture of the ranch, maybe in the springtime, judging by the wildflowers. "I painted them." She had come up behind me. I looked at the paintings a moment longer, and then turned back around. "They're so peaceful," I said. The smile remained intact on her face. "That's what I was trying for," she said. We finished the tour with the kitchen, which smelled wonderful, and a brief glance at the back patio. We turned back into the kitchen, and I wondered about Kate's mother. There had been no mention of her, and I saw no sign of there being another woman in the house. I glanced around one more time, and she guessed what I was wondering about. "My mom isn't here anymore. The West didn't suit her, at least not the ranch country of the West. One day she left us and took the stage to San Francisco. She might still be there, I'm not sure. Dad and I have always loved it here." "You're lucky to have him," I told her. "He's a good man." She nodded. "What about your parents?" I heard the footsteps of the others headed toward the kitchen. "It's a really long story," I said. "Can I tell you another time?" She nodded again, and turned to seat everyone for dinner.

We sat around an old table in the kitchen for dinner, with Jim at the head of the table, Yates and Kate were seated on one side, me at the other end to Kate's right, with Red on the side opposite Yates and Kate. We helped ourselves to roast beef from the ranch, vegetables grown in Kate's garden, and mashed potatoes. I would have enjoyed it immensely, except for the conversation. Yates, I had to admit, was a very entertaining conversationalist. He seemed to have an endless supply of funny stories, half of which I suspected were untrue, and a lot of quick jokes and quips. I could tell that Kate was enjoying his company, and I began to feel pretty uncomfortable. Jim and I chipped in a few sentences only once in a while, and Red sat in complete silence.

Eventually, Carson turned his sights on me. It was instant dislike between us, clearly. "So," he began, "Jim tells me you came here from New York. You think you have any skills for helping out on a ranch?" That came out with a bit of a smirk. "Sure," I said. "I've worked on a ranch before." That took him by surprise, a little. "Where?" "Not too far from here," I said a bit evasively. "I came west with my parents when I was little, but didn't get to stay here when I got a little older." "Near here? Where? Why did you go to New York?" I looked up at him, debating how much to tell him. Jim Randolph leaned in. "Yates," he said, "at my table a man is free to talk about his past as much as he wants to, and no more." Yates swung around to look at Randolph, didn't like the look he saw, and dropped his next question.

Eventually, Carson decided to return to the attack, only a little more subtly. "Well," he said after a while, "you can ride and herd cattle?" I nodded and said nothing else. A smirk formed on his lips. "Anything else that might be useful?" I put down my fork and stared at him. An idea formed in my mind. It was a longshot, but I decided to give it a try. "Sure" I said. "I can repair fence over on that east side pasture if I need to." His gaze was on his plate when I said it, but his head snapped up quickly. Even Red seemed to do a double-take. Yates looked at me through narrowed eyes, his antagonism evident in his look. Eventually he became aware of Kate, looking at him with unspoken questions in her eyes. Yates dropped his gaze back to his plate and he went back to work on finishing his dinner.

The rest of the meal could only be described as uncomfortable, although Jim didn't seem bothered down on his end. Kate made a few efforts at restarting the conversation, but Carson had retreated into an ugly silence. Finally, he and Red excused themselves at about the same time and left. I took my turn at trying to restart the conversation, and father and daughter both responded a bit, but I eventually gave it up. I couldn't tell if Kate was angry at me or simply perplexed by the earlier exchange. I complimented her on the meal and let myself out.

As I went down the path toward the bunk house, I became aware of a low conversation around the side of the ranch house. I turned and walked noiselessly to the corner of the house and looked carefully around the corner. Yates Carson was mounted on his horse, and had moved only a few yards toward the trail back to his ranch. Red was standing next to his horse, and they were talking in low tones. I turned quietly and continued over to the bunk house. Obviously there was more going on there than met the eye. I had some things to think about.

Chapter 6

Kate Randolph awakened suddenly. She glanced toward the window; saw that there was only a little gray light filtering in, so it was early. It seemed exceptionally quiet outside. She lay back in the bed and looked up at the fabric covering her four poster bed and wondered why she had awakened so early. Something about last night was troubling her, and she was having trouble pinpointing the source of her worries. She began to replay the evening in her head.

Oh yes… it was coming back to her now. Chance had made a comment about repairing the eastern fence, and it had obviously touched a nerve with Yates and maybe Red as well. She remembered glancing over at her father; his face had been expressionless. So he hadn't been surprised by it. Beyond that she hadn't been able to tell what he was thinking. Chance's comment had pretty much implied that the Carsons were stealing Randolph cattle. Was that possible? She thought of what she knew about Yates. He was witty and entertaining, and she had found that she enjoyed his company. At times he seemed frivolous, and didn't seem to show much interest in hard work or in building his ranch. That had caused her to shy away when he talked of marriage. She knew her father would be angry if he knew that Yates had proposed. She had decided against the marriage, but didn't want the companionship and enjoyable times to end.

She thought of the older Carson brothers. The middle brother, Caleb, seemed to have a quick temper and didn't show her much respect when she was around. The oldest brother, Jack, was just evil, in her opinion. He was said to have killed several men in gunfights. She knew she could never marry into that family. Still, could Yates have been stealing cattle? She couldn't really picture it. The older brothers, maybe, but she didn't think Yates was capable of it. What did Chance really know about this? Or her father? Would either of them tell her?

She got up and walked to the window. The sky was cloudy and it would be a little cold in the early morning, but she had to know if Yates could be involved in stealing cattle. The idea came to her to dress and ride up to the high pasture, check the fence, and she what she could find on her own. She decided quickly to do so, dressed, and left a note for her father, telling him she had gone on an early morning ride.

In the corral she buttoned up her coat against morning chill of the late spring, saddled her horse, a buckskin mare, and rode out. She glanced at the cattle as she rode through the lower pasture. In a few weeks, as the temperatures rose, they could be moved to the high pasture, where they would find abundant new lush grass and begin to really fatten up. She reached the eastern edge of the lower pasture and took the path to climb to the high pasture.

The morning light was still dim as Kate rode into the high pasture, and there was a bit of morning fog. She rode to the barb wire fence and leaned a bit from the saddle as she looked for any sign of wire that had been cut and repaired. She saw nothing in the first several yards, and it dawned on her that if there had been any cattle stolen, it was likely that it would have happened farther up the line, where there was less chance of being seen. She rode along to the north for perhaps a quarter of a mile, scanning the upper strand of the wire as she went. She began to hear a few rumbles of thunder and anxiously scanned the skies overhead. Violent storms could move in quickly sometimes. She could only hope this wasn't one of those times.

She glanced toward the north, peering through the fog in the dim morning light, then suddenly reined in her horse. At first she doubted her own eyes, but it gradually became clear there were two men standing by the fence, one on each side. Their horses were cropping grass nearby. A few cattle were grazing to one side, four to be exact, on the Randolph property. Kate's glance veered back to the two men at the fence. The posture and shape of the man on her side of the fence was undoubtedly Red. She looked to the other side of the fence, and her heart sunk as she realized it was Yates. She sat indecisively for a moment, and then her horse, sensing the presence of the other two horses, whinnied. Both men whirled and saw her. Yates appeared to be holding a metallic instrument of some kind in his hand.

The shock was gradually being replaced by anger as she realized these two were, in fact, stealing Randolph cattle. She had a moment of indecision, but quickly realized that retreat wasn't an option. She had been seen, and they started to advance toward her. She spurred her horse forward. "So, it's true" she said, riding up to within a few feet of them. "You are cattle thieves. How long?" Her gaze shifted to Yates, who was placing the snips back inside his jacket. "The whole time you've been coming to see me, talking about marriage, have you been stealing my cows that whole time?" She looked back at Red. "How about you? Have you been taking our cows the whole time you've been taking our money?" The two exchanged glances, then Yates looked at her, his eyes narrowed in anger, and she sensed menace in his face. Her anger began to subside and she felt fear for the first time.

She looked at Yates, measured his expression, and realized she had never truly seen what he was like. She gathered the reins and began to back her horse. Yates turned to Red. "Deal with it" he said, and then he turned, mounted his horse, and rode away. Kate tore her gaze from Yates back to Red and saw the gun in his hand. She stopped her horse and watched the gun come level, then closed her eyes and waited for the inevitable. When no shot came after several seconds, she opened her eyes. Red was still holding the gun on her, but he was looking at the ground. She realized, with a glimmer of hope, that he might not be prepared to do this. "You stole some cows" she said. "That doesn't make you a murderer."

Red made his decision. He dropped the barrel of the gun to point at the ground directly in front of the horse and fired as he turned and galloped away. Kate's horse reared immediately, then came down and gathered herself as she began to plunge and run. Kate instinctively yanked both feet from the stirrups and prepared to throw herself off. Her left foot came free, but her right foot was only partially dislodged. She clung to the reins and saddle horn as her horse began to gallop. She made one more effort to dislodge her foot as she was thrown clear. She felt a sharp pain in her right ankle but her foot came free, throwing her to the ground as her horse disappeared from sight. Her breath was knocked out of her when she landed, and she lay where she had fallen, recovering her breath. A bolt of lightning flashed, followed by thunder and the rain came immediately after, falling in sheets within a minute or two.

Kate lay on the ground, shivering in the morning cold after she was drenched almost immediately by the thunderstorm. She looked around for cover from the rain, but there was none to be found around her in the pasture. She looked to the north. The closest cover would be in the trees bordering the pasture on the north. She tried to stand and eventually did struggle to her feet. She took one step with her left foot, but when she tried to step out with the right foot, it buckled and she fell to the ground. The pain was all but unbearable, and clearly the ankle wouldn't support her weight. She could see that it had swollen considerably already. She decided to crawl to the trees, if she could make it. The movement might at least bring the shivering under control. After progressing several yards, she slumped to the ground to rest. The rain fell on her relentlessly and she began to shiver again.

I came out of the bunkhouse in the morning light and looked around. Rumbles of thunder and an occasional flicker of lightning told me rain was coming. I had a vague memory of Red leaving the bunkhouse sometime before morning came, but had assumed he was only going out to answer the call of nature. I had drifted back off to sleep and he wasn't there when I woke up. I saw Jim walking toward the corral and headed over there myself. "Mornin" he said. He was carrying a hammer and a handful of nails. "Got some breakfast on the stove. Go in and grab something to eat, then come on back out and help me shoe a couple horses." I glanced at the house and hesitated. "Kate's gone for a morning ride. No problem with just going on in." He glanced at the sky. "I hope she gets back before this storm sets in."

We made short work of the shoeing. I held their heads while Jim replaced the shoes. They seemed to be very used to the process. Jim gave me a couple tips while he worked and we switched places so I could do the last one. As we worked, the sky overhead darkened and the roll of thunder became more insistent. A spatter of rain began. Jim stepped back and caught up his horse. "I'm going to check on the cattle in the lower pasture and look for Kate" he said. "This storm rolled in awfully fast. Can you check the high pasture for her?" I nodded and headed over to Archie as Jim rode out of the corral.

The skies opened up and the rain came down heavily as I worked my way across the lower pasture, tugging my slicker over my head as I went. I decided, for no particular reason, to work the west side of the high pasture first. I held Archie to a trot and kept my head moving from left to right, calling Kate's name from time to time. Rain was coming down so heavily I couldn't see for more than a few yards. I held the hood of my slicker to keep it from blowing off, squinting my eyes against the rain. I worked my way to the stream cutting across the high pasture with no sign of Kate. I hesitated and debated whether to cross the stream and search clear up to the tree line on the north, or to work my way east along the stream. Archie suddenly swung his head and snorted, and I looked around and saw a saddled, riderless buckskin horse trotting toward us, reins trailing. I nudged Archie in her direction and held up my hand, talking soothingly. She came to a stop and stood quietly while I gathered the reins in my left hand.

We worked our way along the stream to the east fairly slowly and I called Kate's name constantly as we went. I leaned into the wind and the rain, which was falling almost sideways now. The thunder was constant, drowning me out often when I called her name. We moved east for about fifteen minutes and I knew we were nearing the fence along the eastern side of the property. I was renewing my earlier debate about crossing the stream or searching south of the stream along the fence line when I saw someone down on the ground and crawling toward the stream. A second later the long blonde hair told me it was Kate and I touched Archie with the spurs. We galloped the remaining way and I tied the buckskin's reins to the saddle horn as I swung down.

"Kate!" She rolled over in my direction as I ran up to her. "I'm so glad..." The thunder and the wind swept away the rest of her words as I knelt down beside her. Even in the poor light and the rain I could see how pale she was, and she pointed toward her right foot. I turned and looked. It was badly swollen. I couldn't tell if it was a break or a bad sprain. I looked back at her face, and my experience in the army told me she wasn't far from passing out. She was shivering constantly. I gathered her up, carried her over and placed her on Archie's saddle, then swung up behind her. The good news was that I knew we weren't far from shelter and warmth. I told her so, and then urged Archie forward across the stream.

I was much less familiar with the entrance to the cave from the Randolph side of the property. We climbed toward the pine trees and the scattered boulders. I held the reins with one hand and cradled Kate with the other arm as she slumped against me in the saddle. The buckskin trailed along behind us. When I thought we were close to the entrance, I tied the horses to a tree, lifted Kate from the saddle and swung around a few boulders and the rocky wall of a cliff. Luck was with me and I spotted the entrance to the cave shortly. I carried Kate in and set her down on the floor, then began to rummage around in the supplies I had left there. I found the bedroll first, untied it and rolled it open, then pulled it over next to Kate and helped her move over to it. I dug into the supply of firewood and kindling I had left there. I found matches in my knapsack, along with a dry shirt and a pair of pants.

I pulled the firewood and kindling past Kate and near the entrance to the cave. I had a good fire going shortly, after which I found a couple old blankets I spread over Kate. She took in the cave and my campfire efforts quietly, though I could see there were questions she wanted to ask.

I stood back against the wall of the cave and watched as the fire and the extra blankets had their effect. Gradually she stopped shivering and some color returned to her face. She looked at me standing against the wall and patted a spot next to her on the bedroll. "Shared warmth is another way to control the shivering." I didn't seem to have any objections to that, so I went over and sat down next to her on the bedroll. "Thank you" she said quietly and leaned against me for a moment. "Do you mind if I ask you some questions now?" "Go ahead" I answered.

She turned to face me a little more, then leaned back on the bedroll. I pulled another old blanket under her head to serve as a pillow. "What is this place? And how did you know about it? You found it pretty quickly." I nodded and studied her face. "I used to be your neighbor" I said simply. "I found it when I was a kid. I dragged some supplies up here before I started work at your place because I thought it might come in handy someday. I had no idea that day would come so soon." She looked at me, searching my face, and I saw the comprehension dawn in her eyes. "The O'Reillys. So you're Boy-o." I nodded. "I guess I never knew your real name" she said. I nodded again.

Kate laid her head back down on the blanket and stared at the cave ceiling. "No wonder" she said. Now it was my turn to ask questions. "What do you mean?" "Well," she said, "Dad is very slow to accept strangers and very careful about who he trusts. He seemed to take to you immediately and that is very unlike him. Now I know why." I laid on my side on the bedroll and cradled my head in my hand. "Will you tell me how you came to be unhorsed? I assume you hurt your ankle when you were thrown from the horse. Was it the storm?" She shook her head and I could see a flash of anger in her eyes. "I woke up thinking about your comment last night about mending the eastern fence. It struck a nerve with Yates and I started wondering if he could really be stealing cows. I rode out this morning to see if I could see signs of the fence being cut and repaired. I stumbled across Yates and Red cutting the fence and stealing cows, and they saw me. I didn't see much choice other than confronting them." She stared into the fire. "I was so angry."

She finished the story, telling me about Red firing into the ground and spooking her horse. When she finished, I felt the anger building inside of me. It sounded like she could have easily been dragged to death by the runaway horse. She shifted her position on the bedroll and I saw the pain in her eyes when she moved her right leg. I got up and went back into the cave, picking up a couple of old pans and a pair of pants and an old shirt. I went back to Kate and dropped the clothes beside her. "I'm going out to get some cold water from the stream. I think if we get some cold water on the ankle it might take down the swelling. While I'm gone, I'd suggest you change into the dry clothes. If you need help, I'll help." What I had just said started to sink in a little, and I glanced at Kate, embarrassed. She looked at me speculatively. I think I blushed. "You need the dry clothes to fight off the chill" I offered lamely, my voice trailing away. For the first time that day, a smile appeared on her face and she laughed at my obvious discomfort. "I can manage" she said. "Down, boy."

I grabbed the empty pots and beat a retreat from the cave, pulling my slicker over my head as I went out. The thunder and lightning seemed to have subsided, but the rain still lashed my face as I came out from the cover of the cave. I started to untie Archie, but then realized I wouldn't be able to carry both pans of water and keep them from spilling while I rode. I bent my head against the torrents of rain and walked down to the stream, which was already almost twice its normal size. I filled both pans and made the walk back up the hill and into the cave. The warmth of the fire was wonderful when I re-entered.

I found another old shirt and tore it into strips. I came back over to Kate and placed the pans of water beside the bedroll. "I need to lift your right leg over my knee and get some cold water on that ankle" I told her. "It might hurt a little." She made no complaint as I slowly lifted her leg and cradled the calf over my knee. I dipped a rag into the ice cold water and squeezed it over her ankle, gently rubbing with the rag. She drew a quick breath at the touch of the cold water, but lay still as I repeatedly dipped the rag and applied the cold water to her ankle. I kept it up for ten or fifteen minutes until the water was more lukewarm than cold. I pushed the pans aside, put her leg back down on the bedroll and sat back. Kate propped herself up on her elbows and tried a few slow movements with the right leg. "I think that's better" she said. "Where did you learn to do that?" I picked up the pans, poured the water outside the cave and came back. "In the army" I told her. "The medic in our group swore by applying cold to swelling. He used ice if he had it, cold water otherwise."

"You were in the army. During the war." The question came out as a statement and I nodded. She laid back down on the bedroll and patted the spot beside her again. "Come tell me more about what you did after you left Cimarron." I lay down beside her and she curled her arm around mine. I began to tell her about my trip back to New York, about my aunt and uncle, my time in the war and my experiences working at the Metropolitan Hotel. Sometimes she asked questions and I answered them with as much detail as I could remember. Gradually the questions came less and less often. I continued telling the stories until the deep, regular breathing told me she had fallen asleep. I stayed where I was on the bedroll, turning over in my mind what had happened to her that morning. How much trouble could she and her father be in for when the Carson brothers all realized they had been identified as cattle thieves? My mind turned it over and over, trying to formulate a plan. Eventually I drifted off to sleep also.

When I came to, the storm had passed and the sun was beginning to break through the clouds. I stood outside the cave and looked around me. It seemed unlikely that either Yates Carson or Red had returned to the area, but we needed to be careful, all the same. I heard stirring inside the cave and came back to find Kate on her feet but leaning against the wall of the cave. I put out the fire and looked over at her. "We should get back" I told her. "Can you ride?" "I'm sure I can" she told me, but didn't move away from where she stood against the wall. I walked over and picked her up in my arms. "It isn't far to the horses" I said, and we walked out of the cave, around the corner and down the hill a short way. I lifted her up and put her in the buckskin's saddle and reached out to untie the reins. When I turned to give her the reins, I brushed against the right ankle and I heard a sharp intake of breath.

"I'm sorry!" I handed her the reins and stepped back, feeling clumsy. "Don't worry about it" she said. She leaned over a little and crooked her finger, beckoning me to come closer. I stepped forward and she leaned a little farther, placing her lips against my ear. "I could have walked down to the horses, but it was more fun this way" she whispered. I looked up in surprise and watched the smile spread across her face. I searched my mind for what to say, but I didn't seem to be thinking of anything. Finally I chuckled and went over to climb up on Archie. I swung Archie around and looked back at her. "I like the way you think" I said. Then I turned Archie toward the ranch house and we headed home.

Chapter Seven

The sun was nearly directly overhead as we rode out, and I was surprised to realize it was somewhere around noon. So much had happened, and yet I was surprised to see that it was this late in the day. The heavy clouds overhead had begun to break up, and patches of blue sky were showing through. Kate and I rode side by side, and she reassured me several times that the pain in her ankle wasn't too much to keep going. She seemed anxious to get back to the house.

Shortly after we crossed the stream and worked our way toward the southern edge of the high pasture, I saw another rider coming from the lower pasture, headed in our direction. My hand dropped instinctively toward the Colt on my hip, a movement not lost on Kate. She reached out and put a restraining hand on my wrist. "It's Dad," she said. "I recognize his hat and coat." I relaxed immediately and we continued on down until we met up with him. There was grim concern in his eyes and his glance kept dropping down to Kate's ankle as we rode up. I let her ride ahead to him.

"It's OK. Chance came along at just the right time and helped me through a bad spot. Let's just keep riding down to the house." Jim hesitated, then nodded and fell along beside her as they turned back toward home. I trailed along a few paces behind while she told him the story. He glanced back in some surprise when she told him about the cave where I'd taken her, and turned back and rode in silence the rest of the way to the corral. He helped support her weight to walk her into the house. I stood near the doorway just inside the house, twisting my hat in my hands while he helped her over to the sofa, put some pillows under her ankle and brought her some water. He came over, took my elbow and guided me out to the porch, closing the door quietly behind us. The concern in his eyes had given way to deep anger.

We stood outside for a few moments while he gathered his thoughts and stared out at the corral. Finally, he spoke: "First of all Chance, I'm deeply beholden to you for looking after Kate like you did." His mouth opened and closed a couple times with no words spoken while he gathered his thoughts. "I had my doubts about Red, you know that. I didn't think he was capable of this. Yates and Red have both been pegged as cattle thieves now. Nobody's going to take their word over Kate's. That makes them dangerous and puts us in their sights." He fell silent and thought for a while longer. "I need to ask a favor," he said at length.

"Name it." I found myself scanning over his shoulder while we talked, looking for any movement out in the yard. Jim went back in the house and conversed with Kate in low tones for a few minutes while I kept up my watch on the corral, bunkhouse and yard. Jim returned, shaking his head slightly. "Well, I need her to see the doctor, but she's saying she wants to stay in the house today and see how it is tomorrow. There's a doctor that comes through Cimarron two or three days a week. Doc Chapman, he has an office near the hotel. He should be in the area now. I'd like you to ride in, see if you can find him, ask him to come out to the ranch and check that ankle. If you can't find him or he's out on a call, see if you can leave word at the hotel that we'll be coming in tomorrow morning to see him. Can you do that for me?" I nodded and started toward the bunkhouse and corral, but Jim stopped me with a hand on my arm. "I'm sure she'd like to talk to you for a minute before you leave."

Why hadn't I thought of that? I turned and went back inside. Kate had her ankle propped up on a couple of pillows and was leaning back against the edge of the sofa. She was still pale, but I could see the color in her face was much better and she held her hand out to me. I took her hand and sat on the edge of the sofa. "I wanted you to know how much I appreciate what you did for me. I've had to pretty much rely on myself out here, so it was really special the way you took care of me. I won't forget." She gave me a quick hug, and then leaned back against the sofa. "Be careful on your way to town. Come back in and see me when you're back." "I will," I said. I patted her hand and stood up. "And I'll be sure to arrange for the doctor to see you." I trotted out to the bunkhouse and picked up my Winchester before heading to the corral and climbing up on Archie. The miles back to Cimarron passed quickly and uneventfully. I wondered where Red and Yates Carson had gone.

I remembered the doctor's office from my weeks in Cimarron, though I hadn't seen him around town all that often. A knock on the door and a quick glance through the window told me he wasn't in his office. I stepped in to the hotel lobby next door and was told at the desk that the doctor was making a call or two at ranches in the area and wasn't expected back until sometime tonight. I left the message about Jim and Kate coming in the next morning, and the clerk promised me he would deliver the message.

I stepped out of the hotel and looked up and down the street, wondering whether I should go on back to the ranch or try to pick up some information on whether or not anyone in town knew about what had happened to Kate that morning. There didn't seem to be any unusual activity in the street. I glanced up and down, noticing only that the mining supply store seemed to be closing up. I knew the owner only by his first name, Tim, from his occasional stops at the saloon. I saw a few signs about sale items, and a few things scattered on the front porch. Tim appeared in the front door, waved, and dropped a few more items on the porch. I thought about the brief side trip I'd made into the Sangre de Cristo Mountains on my way down from Denver and decided to drop in for a few minutes. I crossed the street and entered the front door.

"Hey". Tim gave me a friendly smile and continued packing up his supplies. "You leaving Cimarron?" I asked. He nodded. "Not enough business for me in this neck of the woods," he replied. "I'm moving the store up to Denver. I think there'll be enough mining activity up there to make a go of the business." I nodded and watched him for a while. I thought about the rumors of gold in the mountains to the north, and I thought of how little money I had; of how little I had to offer a woman like Kate.

"Tell me," I said eventually. "If you found gold around here, how would you go about mining it?" Tim stopped and looked at me with open curiosity, but he avoided asking the obvious questions he was probably thinking. He stopped his work and took a seat on a stool near the front of the shop. "OK, tell me more about it. Would it be a quartz deposit on the side of a cave or mountain wall, would it be gold in a stream bed, what?" I thought for a minute and realized I didn't exactly know. "Probably a quartz deposit on a cave wall," I said eventually. Tim absorbed that one and thought for a minute.

"First, of course, you'll need an axe to knock down the quartz." As he talked he began to pull out the items he'd mentioned and stacked them on the floor. "Then, you would need something to crush the rock and separate the gold." He pulled out a fairly large mortar and pestle and set that in the middle of the floor. I looked at it with some surprise. "Best thing for crushing the rock. You can get pretty efficient with it in a hurry. Then, you need a screen mesh to separate the rock sediment from the gold ore." He set a large screen in a wooden box in the middle of the floor. I walked around to take a closer look at the screen. It was a pretty fine mesh set into a wooden frame. "How does this work?" I asked. Tim picked up the screen and did a brief demonstration. "You put the rock pieces and sediment on the screen, then sift and shake it. The sediment falls through the screen. The gold stays on top." I nodded.

"If you have a river or stream to work with, you can use a sluice box and run the water through to separate the gold," he continued. "Do you think you'd be able to do that?" I thought about how vulnerable I would be to Indian attack if I knelt in a stream to pan gold, and I couldn't imagine staying out in the open that long with no one to watch my back. I shook my head no and decided I would concentrate on working the cave walls with the axe.

"OK," he continued. "Well, you would have some gold ore at this point, somewhat separated from the rock. You could pack that out and have it processed in town." He thought for a minute. "How light would you have to travel? Would you have a pack animal to carry the crushed ore out of there?" I thought about that one for a minute and told him I would want to travel as light as possible. He went to the back of the store, opened a few cabinets and came back with a bottle of some kind of liquid, some heavy work gloves and a large metal pan. "You could use these to crudely process the gold where you are, and you won't have to pack out as much sediment and crushed rock." He showed me the bottle—it was mercury. "You can take a cloth and spread the mercury on the bottom of the pan. Be sure you don't get any on your hands. Pour the gold ore you have on the bottom of the pan and scrape out the gold after it mixes with the mercury. Scrape gold and traces of mercury into a brick or a ball. It'll be heavy, but it is a lot purer form of gold to pack out with you. Gives you less stuff you're trying to pack out if you're in hostile country, and might keep some thieves from following you and stealing the gold before you can cash it in. You want to buy this stuff?" He waved his hand at the pile of supplies he had stacked in the middle of the floor.

I thought for a minute and nodded. "I want it," I said. Can you hold it for me for a day or two and I'll come back to pay you and pick it up." We shook hands. "Deal," he said. "And if you're ever in Denver with some gold ore you've mined, look me up. I can help you cash it in without attracting too many crooks and thieves."

I turned to go but hesitated in the doorway, trying to frame one last question in my mind. How much gold would I need if I wanted to really make a good start in life? What would it take to buy a ranch like the one my dad and I had, get some cattle and get going with my own place? I picked a number out of the air and looked back at Tim. "Let's say I wanted to come out with $5,000 in gold. How many of those bricks you described would I need?" Tim stopped and turned that question over in his mind for a while. "Let's say three or four bricks if the gold is pretty good quality."

I shook his hand and walked out to the porch. I figured I could pick up those supplies after Tim got them together and store them up in the cave until I decided to use them. I looked over at the doctor's office and saw the door was still closed. A glance up and down the street told me there still wasn't much happening in town. Time for me to be getting back.

Shadows were lengthening across the yard and the corral when I got back to the ranch. I announced myself several times as I rode up, and I found Jim sitting in a corner of the porch, cradling his rifle. I joined him on the porch and Kate came out to sit with us. I told them I had left a message with Doc Chapman and he should be expecting our visit in the morning. There had been no sign of Yates

Carson or Red in town. Jim handed me the rifle and patted me on the shoulder as he went inside. "I'm going to get us some dinner," he announced. The door shut softly behind him.

Kate moved over next to me on the porch and I helped her prop her ankle up on another chair. "How's it feeling?" I asked as I sat back down beside her. She rested her hand on top of mine. "It's doing better. I think the swelling is down a little more and I'm hoping it's just a bad sprain. Doc Chapman will get me fixed up." We sat companionably for a while in the silence, but I kept my eyes scanning for any movement in the yard. "What do you think is going to happen?" she asked eventually. I shook my head as I considered it. "Best case scenario, Yates Carson and Red were small time cattle thieves acting on their own without the brothers, and they've left town for good. I'm hoping for that one. Worst case scenario, all three Carson brothers move against us when they get word of what happened this morning. It would be a good idea if you and Jim pay a visit to the sheriff in town after you've seen the doctor tomorrow." She absorbed what I'd said thoughtfully, then eventually laid her head against my shoulder as we watched darkness fall across the ranch yard. A few minutes later Jim told us he had some dinner ready and we went inside.

Morning found me back on the trail to Cimarron, riding point for Jim and Kate, who were following in the wagon. We paused at the place where the trail branched off to the Carson ranch, looking at the tracks in the trail. None of them appeared to be fresh, so there were still no clues as to the whereabouts of Red and Yates. I hoped once again that they had just moved on. We completed the trip to Cimarron without incident. I surveyed the streets while Jim and Kate went into the doctor's office. Everything still seemed pretty quiet, but I knew the best place to get information would be at the saloon. I rode over, tied Archie to the rail and went inside. Sam motioned me to a corner table as soon as I went in. We sat down and Sam glanced up as a young guy with a mop of blonde hair came up. Sam pointed at him. "This is your replacement, Chance. My sister's kid, Mike. I'm teaching him the saloon business." Mike grinned and shook my hand. "We don't need anything Mike," he said. "Just keep an eye on the bar for me."

Sam swung back around to face me. "You got trouble" he said shortly. I looked at him and waited for an explanation. "Word is that Yates Carson says you accused him of cattle rustling. He plans to call you out in town and kill you." I stared at him and tried to process what he was telling me. Finally I spoke. "I did drop some big hints that he might be a rustler. And it turns out he is." I told him what had happened the previous morning. Sam nodded. "Sounds about right." I traced a pattern on the table with my finger. "Even if he manages to kill me" I said, "Kate and Jim still know he's a cattle rustler. It doesn't solve that problem." Sam shrugged. He's a hothead and a fool" he said eventually. "I doubt he's really thought it through that far."

I leaned back in my chair and thought about the choices I had. None of them sounded very good. "What about the sheriff?" I asked. "Has he heard about this and is he around?" "He has" Sam answered. "He rode out to the Carson ranch this morning to talk to Yates and try to calm things down. He'll probably be looking for you too. Mostly he likes to keep things quiet and wants to stop this before it gets out of hand. I don't think Yates is going to talk to him though. He'll be more likely to avoid the sheriff and come to town looking for you." Another thought struck me. "What about Red? Has anybody seen him or heard what he's doing?" Sam shook his head. "I hadn't heard about Red being involved in this until you just told me. I'd watch my back if I were you, though. He doesn't strike me as a man who likes a fair fight."

I sat back in my chair and my hand dropped involuntarily to the Colt I had strapped to my hip.

"What about the other two Carson brothers? Where do they stand with this?" Sam leaned forward a little. "You might have caught a break there. Word is they're out of town." I nodded. "Anything else you can tell me?" Sam put a toothpick in his mouth while he thought about it. "All three brothers fancy themselves gun hands, but the oldest one, Jack, is probably the only one who can make that claim. Middle brother is named Caleb. He's probably been in a scrape or two, but he isn't as salty as Jack. You've met Yates. He's more talk than anything else, but don't take him lightly. All three have probably been on the wrong side of the law at some time. Don't trust any of them to fight fair. They'll try to trick you or bushwhack you if they can." He looked out through the window and pushed back his chair. "Sit tight for a minute. I'll go out and check the street. I'll let you know if there's anything you need to know about out there."

I sat at the table and waited while Sam went outside. I hadn't envisioned it coming to a head this quickly, nor had I thought I would be target number one. I had no intention of avoiding it, though. If he wanted to bring the fight to me, I would have to deal with it now. A few people glanced at me curiously, but no one came over to talk. I wondered how much the word had spread in town about this. Footsteps approached and I looked up to see Sam standing by the table. "He's here. He's in the main street in front of the hotel, saying he wants to see you out there." I stood up and double checked my pistol. "Don't let him trick you," Sam said. "Watch his eyes. You'll see it in the eyes if he's going for his gun."

I took a deep breath, turned around and walked out through the batwing doors of the saloon.

Chapter 8

Sam remained at the table by the window as he watched Chance Reilly leave the saloon. He thought about what he'd just told Chance about watching his back and not counting on a fair fight. It remained in his thoughts and nagged at the back of his mind as he went about tending the bar and washing a few beer glasses. It seemed a little unlike Yates Carson to ride into town and challenge Chance to an even fight on the street. Sam mopped the bar absentmindedly... nobody had seen Red since the incident yesterday morning. A couple customers came in and headed for the bar, but Sam served them quickly, still lost in his thoughts.

Finally he made up his mind and motioned his nephew over. "Mike," he yelled. "Watch the bar." Sam reached under the bar, picked up his shotgun and let himself out the back door of the saloon.

He stopped outside the door, checked to make sure the shotgun was loaded, and thought in terms of that unfair fight he'd been talking to Chance about. If Carson planned some kind of ambush and he had stationed himself in front of the hotel at the north end of town, Red or whoever else was in on an ambush would be farther north on a roof or in a side alley so the shot would come from the same direction. Sam turned north and started working his way down the path that ran in back of the stores and shops on the main street. The town didn't really have much in terms of side streets—just the alleys that existed between the shops. Sam worked his way steadily along, easing past the alley openings as he came to them, shotgun at the ready. There was a hum of voices each time he came to an opening between the buildings, and he realized that no one seemed to be entering or leaving the town.

As he worked his way north to the hotel and the buildings to either side of it, Sam saw that people had gathered along the street in front of the buildings. He shook his head and thought about the stupidity of standing where you could be hit by a stray bullet. He glanced briefly into the alleys between buildings on both sides of the hotel, but people were standing at the front of both alleys, looking toward the street, blocking any potential ambush. Sam kept going, nearing the edge of town. At last, in an alleyway between buildings on the far north side of town, he found what he was looking for. Red was kneeling at the front of the alley, rifle extended out in front of him. Sam turned the corner and paused while he assessed his next move. Was Red the only one waiting in ambush, or could there be more?

Finally Sam began to ease his way quietly forward. Time could be of the essence. Red was concentrating on the scene in front of him, which helped. Sam knew he wasn't as cat-footed as he used to be, but he slowly and carefully closed the distance between them. Just a few more feet until the shotgun would be at its most effective. When he had closed to within a few steps, Sam could see that Red's head had turned slightly and he seemed to be focused on sounds behind him. Red abruptly lunged to his feet, swinging his rifle around as he turned. Sam jumped forward the last couple steps and jammed the barrel of the shotgun into Red's back before he turn any farther. Red froze where he was, but Sam could see he still had the rifle in his hands. Red hesitated, and Sam prodded his back with the barrel. "That's a shotgun barrel you're feeling," Sam said in a conversational tone. "Don't make me prove I know what to do with it."

Red dropped the rifle into the alley and stood motionless. Sam could see the pistol on his hip. "Hands up in the air where I can see them" he said. He backed away a few feet as Red raised his hands above his head. "OK, now turn around slowly." If Red was surprised to see it was Sam holding the shotgun, he didn't show it. His expression didn't change. Sam motioned to the pistol and belt around Red's waist. "Now unbuckle slowly and toss the whole belt over here. Be sure you don't touch that pistol." Red seemed to hesitate, looking at the shotgun and distance between them. "You're welcome to try" Sam said. "If you do, I'll scatter you all over the alley with this here shotgun. I doubt anybody will mind." Red slowly unbuckled the belt and tossed it at Sam's feet.

"So," Sam said, staring at him. "Cattle thief, dry-gulcher, and you don't mind seeing a woman get dragged by her horse, neither. I'm thinking you need to leave town. When I'm done telling my story, they'll be looking for a tree limb for you. I'm doing you a favor letting you leave. Where's your horse?" Red's eyes had narrowed in anger, but he made no move other than to point at the building next to them. "Tied to the rail in back." Sam motioned again with the shotgun. "Go over and get on him." Red looked at his pistol lying on the ground, then back at Sam. "You going to send me out in Injun country without my gun?" Sam considered that for a moment, then reached down and picked up the gun. He opened the chamber and emptied it. Then he reached down and picked up a single bullet. He tossed the pistol and the bullet over to Red. "Here," he said. "You try to load that bullet before you're out of town, you'll hear from my shotgun." Red picked up the gun and the single bullet. "And my rifle?" he asked. Sam's gaze went from the rifle lying on the ground to the street and back. "I've seen how you like to use that rifle.   It can stay here with me. I'll make sure it gets a good home" Sam told him. Red put the gun in one pocket and the bullet in the other. "What if I run into Apaches between here and the next town?" Sam shook his head. "If that happens, I'd suggest you make that bullet count" he advised.

Red moved slowly around Sam, giving wide berth to the shotgun. Sam followed him back to the end of the alley, and then watched as Red mounted up. Red glanced back at Sam as if to say something, then seemed to think better of it. He rode out of town without looking back. Sam walked back to the alley, bent down and picked up the remaining bullets lying on the ground. He straightened up, walked over and reached down to pick up the rifle. He stood up and had turned to go back to the saloon before he heard the sound of gunfire coming from the street.

I stopped outside the saloon door and let my eyes adjust to the brighter light outside, still a little stunned at developments. My practice sessions in the woods with the gun might come in handy a lot sooner than I thought. I pulled the pistol from the holster and spun the chamber, making sure it was loaded. A couple people stood near the saloon eyeing me curiously, but I could see that most were up the street, congregating at or near the hotel. I turned and started in that direction.

A familiar figure separated from the crowd and walked toward me, and I saw that it was Jim Randolph. I stopped and let him come to me. He crossed the street, shaking his head. "Have you heard about Yates Carson?" he asked. I nodded, glancing around as I did, wondering where Kate was. He followed my glance. "She's still in the doc's office. She just twisted the ankle. Need to stay off it for a few more days and then she'll probably get around with a cane for a little while after that. I told her she needs to stay inside if she doesn't want to stop a stray bullet." He sighed. "She wanted to talk to Carson, so I went out to him and asked if he would take off his gun, come in the doc's office with me and talk to Kate. That was a no. I think he's crazy enough to believe he can clear his name in this whole business if he shoots you." I looked down the street. "Still no sign of his brothers or Red, right?" Jim nodded. "That's right." He held out a hand to stop me as I started for the hotel. "I feel like this is my fight, not yours." I hesitated for only a moment. "You already tried to talk some sense into him. Now I guess he's made it my fight." I moved out to the center of the street and continued toward the hotel.

I saw a group of people gathered in front of the hotel, and as I walked toward them, they stepped away from the street and up to the boardwalk in front of the stores. Then I saw Yates, wearing a tied down gun holster and standing in the center of the street. I glanced left and right to make sure the sun wasn't in my eyes, then slowed down and stopped about 25 feet away from him. The silence was almost complete. I could hear a door quietly opening and closing behind me. No one was talking. I couldn't tell if he was entirely sober or not. He seemed pretty steady on his feet, but was staring at me with a bit of a crazed expression. Small things etched themselves on my mind as we stood there. He was wearing a straw hat that sat a little off center on his head. His shirt had double flaps over the pockets with oversized copper snaps. He seemed a little disheveled, like maybe he'd fallen from his horse on the way into town. His eyes burned into me. I waited, and finally he spoke.

"You called me a cattle thief." It was a statement, not a question. "I raised the issue" I agreed. "You didn't do anything to improve your image yesterday. What were you doing at the fence line with Red yesterday morning?" He hadn't expected me to go on the offensive, and it set him back a little. He looked a bit uncertain for the first time, and he shifted his feet and paused. He glanced briefly around him, seeming to realize for the first time that he had an audience. "You can go," I offered. "You can get on your horse and ride out of town right now. It doesn't have to come to this." He wavered for just a moment, and then swung his eyes back in my direction and I knew he was too far in to back down. "You're a dead man." His hand hovered near his gun, but his eyes weren't focused on me just yet. I shrugged. "Maybe I am and maybe I'm not. Is it worth it?" His eyes snapped up and locked in on my chest, and then his gun hand moved. His gun came out and began to level, but mine was already clear. I felt it jump in my hand, and the snap over his left front shirt pocket disappeared when the bullet drove into him. His body twisted and his feet seemed to fly out from under him. I stepped forward and to my left as I readied the next shot, but I could see there wasn't any point. He lay still in the dust of the street, the gun on the ground beside him. His knees were buckled and he seemed to be in an oddly twisted position. I walked up to him slowly, gun still ready, but then Doc Chapman pushed in front of me and knelt over him. After a moment he glanced up at me. "He's dead."

I stopped and pushed my gun back into the holster, trying to absorb the enormity of what had just happened. Nobody was coming near me, and I seemed to stand by myself in the center of the street while most stayed on the boardwalk. A few walked and stood over the body briefly. I looked up and saw Kate standing in front of the doctor's office. Her face was completely white and her eyes looked dark and huge by contrast. After a moment Jim Randolph came through the crowd and began to move toward me. Additional movement on my left caught my eye, and I saw Sam coming from the alley between two stores, carrying his shotgun. I stared at him questioningly. "Bit of a long story" he said briefly. "We need to get you off the street. We don't need those brothers coming around right now." Jim joined us and took my arm, steering me off the street. "We'll wait for the sheriff in his office. I'll be the first one to tell him you were provoked and tried to end it without gunfire." He glanced to his side and motioned toward Yates Carson's gun, still lying in the street. "Sam," he said. "Can you bring the gun? It will help to have proof he fired it."

I stared at Jim, but moved along with him toward the sheriff's office. "Did he fire? I can't remember it." Jim nodded. "He got off a shot, but it was too late and too low." He steered me into the office and sat me down. "You're shaking a little now" he observed. "It's an unsettling thing, to draw your gun on a man. Just take your time and breathe deep. I'd get you a little drink to settle you down, but probably better if you haven't been drinking when the sheriff gets here."

I stayed in the chair and replayed the whole confusing scene in my head. I didn't see how it could have come out any differently. Sam came in, laid Carson's gun on the table and sat down next to me. Nobody said anything for several minutes. Finally I looked over at Jim. "Kate looked... horrified" I said eventually. Jim nodded. "It was an ugly thing to see. Give her some time to come to grips with it. She'll know you tried to settle it more peacefully. Just give her a little time." I nodded and stared at the table in front of me.

Finally I heard boots coming toward the office, the door opened, and Sheriff Stanton came in. He walked over to the table and held out his hand. "First, you need to give me your gun" he said, not unkindly. I handed it over without a word; he took it from me and sat down at the table, clearly gathering his thoughts. I wondered what the future held for me now.

Chapter Nine

Morning light filtered slowly through the bars of the Cimarron jail cell. I lay on the bunk and tried to make sense of the last 24 hours. The door to the cell was open. The sheriff had made clear that he didn't consider me a prisoner. His concern was the other two Carson brothers, and the fight that could erupt in town if they returned and came after me. I could hear him snoring lightly out in the front room of the jail. He had stayed the night to prevent them or anyone else storming the jail to get me. He had wanted me to leave town yesterday in the name of keeping the peace. Jim and Sam had argued in my behalf for a long time, but the sheriff had the final word and he wanted me out of town. He'd told me I could return in a year if the Carsons were no longer around.

I rolled over and faced the wall of the cell and sorted through my options. I didn't really have a home to return to. I had hoped that my home would be Cimarron and the Randolph ranch. Jim had made it clear that I was welcome to return, but discouraged me on the idea of doing so against the sheriff's wishes, and I had to agree with him on that one. He had agreed to return with Kate to see me before I left today. I watched a spider weaving his web through the bars of the jail window. My thoughts returned to what I would do now. I had not much of anything to call my own, with only a little in the way of cash. It seemed to me that I needed a stake. I needed something to help me buy my own place and put down some roots. With that, my thoughts returned to my conversation from a couple days ago with Tim in the mining store, and the talk about gold in the Sangre de Cristo Mountains. Maybe I could do some prospecting in those mountains for a while, find enough to stake me to a start somewhere, and start again. It seemed as good a plan as any. I rolled over and got to my feet.

The sound of the doorknob turning stopped me as I reached the door to the cell, and my hand dropped automatically to my side. The gun wasn't there, of course. The sheriff had taken that. The door opened and Sheriff Stanton came in, carrying coffee and some breakfast. He set them down on the table and invited me to join him. He gave me a couple minutes to eat a little and have some coffee, and then began to reiterate what he'd told me yesterday. He expected the remaining two Carson brothers to return and he wanted me gone today. I nodded and glanced up at him. "What about the Randolphs? Do you think they are safe from the Carsons?" The sheriff put his coffee down and hesitated. "I'll help them if they need help," he said finally. I could see the worry in his eyes, but said nothing. He waited for me to finish eating, and then nodded toward a bowl of water in front of a mirror. "You can clean up for a few minutes over there," he said. "The Randolphs will be here in a few minutes to talk to you."

I splashed some water in the bowl and began to go through the motions of washing and shaving, thinking about what I would say to Jim and Kate, and what direction I wanted the conversation to go. I knew that I had to leave. I could only hope to leave the door open for a return, and I hoped Kate would look forward to that possibility. I needed a home and a place to settle, and I desperately hoped this could be it.

When I had finished shaving, I went back to sit down at the table in the front room of the jail. The sheriff, I could see, was sitting outside the jail. It looked like he had a shotgun in his lap. After a few minutes, I could hear footsteps on the boardwalk outside, then Jim and Kate Randolph came through the door. I looked at Kate, trying to make eye contact, but she only glanced at me as she came over and sat down beside me. Jim took the chair opposite. I glanced around the table and decided that nobody had been able to get much sleep last night. A few long moments passed, and nobody seemed to have much to say. Jim finally cleared his throat and began.

"Chance, we have loved having you with us. I... we... felt like you were almost part of our family, with ties to the past and the future..." his voice trailed off for a moment. "We would love to have you back, as soon as this thing can be cleared up, but..." he searched for words again. "Right now, I think you should go, like the sheriff says." I nodded and stared at the table, then glanced up at Kate. I saw both tears and confusion in her eyes. I cleared my throat and stared back down at the table. "I know, Jim" I said. I'll be riding out today." Jim nodded and the silence settled in again over the table. Finally I glanced back up at him. "Could you give me a few minutes to talk to Kate?" Jim pushed his chair back and stood. "Take as much time as you need." He glanced at Kate. "I'll be outside when you're ready."

The sound of the front door shutting filtered back to us at the table. I pulled my chair around to sit next to Kate, put my hand over hers where it lay on the table. "I know that was awfully hard to see yesterday." She pulled away from me. "I saw the whole thing," she said. "I saw you both standing there, I saw the guns come up, and I heard the shots." I looked up and could see the tears coursing down her cheeks. "I saw Yates fall, and I saw you still standing there. I looked back at Yates and I knew he was dead." She wiped the tears away from her cheeks and her hands settled back in her lap. "Part of me knows that you only defended yourself. The other part of me knows that I saw you kill Yates yesterday. I..." she lapsed into silence.

I sat for a moment, both of us staring at the table. I tried another tack. "You can talk to Sam" I said. "He found Red waiting in ambush for me. He'd have shot me down with his rifle before Yates and I ever had it out."

She looked me in the eye for the first time that morning. "I talked to Sam, "she said. "He told me what you just said and I believe him. But I don't believe Yates would have been a part of that. I think Red may have done that without Yates ever knowing." Her eyes shifted away as she said that, and I knew she was having trouble figuring out just what she believed about the whole incident. "Did you see Yates glancing back over his shoulder when he braced me in the street?" I asked. "What do you think he was waiting for?" Her eyes flared and she shook her head. I knew this conversation was going backwards. "He wouldn't have done that." There was finality in her voice this time. I could see she had blocked out the incident from yesterday, when Yates would have let Red kill her at the fence line.

I knew I had to let this one go, so I changed the subject. She would sort this one out in time. Unfortunately, I didn't have time on my side. "I'll be leaving today," I said finally. She looked up and nodded. "I'm truly sorry to see you go," she said. "I'll miss you. We'll both miss you." Well, I thought, that was something. I stood and walked over to the sheriff's desk, then came back with a pencil and a piece of paper. I wrote something on the paper, folded it and gave it to her. She took the paper, but looked at me instead of trying to read it. "What is this?"

"It's an address where you can reach me if you need to. It's a hotel in Denver. I don't think I'm headed there directly, but I'll be there before too much time goes by, and I'll check for a letter. If you need me, just let me know and I'll be here just as fast as I can come." She put the note in the pocket of her skirt, then stood and wrapped an arm around my shoulders. She rested her head on mine for a second, and then brushed my cheek with her lips. "I know you will," she said. "I'll be in touch if I need help. Or maybe I'll just be in touch because the coast is clear and you can come back." The door closed softly behind her.

The door opened and closed again, and Sheriff Stanton was back in the office. He crossed the room, then opened and closed a drawer. He came over to me and held out my gun. "There are no bullets in it," he said. "I assume you have more in your pack?" I took the gun, slid it into my holster and nodded. "Just wait till you're out of town to load it." He extended his hand and I shook it. "No hard feelings?" he asked. "I'm just trying to keep the peace." "No hard feelings" I agreed. I crossed to the door. "I'm going to see Tim for a while at the mining store, then I'm leaving" I said. He waved and sat down in his chair. "Just be gone before dark." I paused at the door. "What if the other two Carson brothers come after Jim and Kate?" There was a long silence while I waited. Finally the answer came back. "I'll do what I need to do." It wasn't much of an answer, but it looked like it was the only one I would get. I opened the door and went on out.

The Cimarron streets seemed pretty empty as I walked away from the jail. One or two people seemed to take an extra look at me as I went by, or maybe I just imagined it. I crossed the street and walked into Tim's Mining Supply store. The shelves seemed mostly empty now. Tim glanced up as the door swung shut, then nodded and walked over after he recognized me. "I heard you had a bit of trouble yesterday" he said. I grinned ruefully. "A bit" I agreed. Tim pointed at a pile of things on the floor in one corner. "Those are yours" he told me.

I walked over and sorted through the things I saw there. He'd set out a shovel, a pickaxe, a fairly large box covered with mesh webbing, a mortar and pestle, and a bottle of liquid. I held up the bottle and looked at him questioningly. "Mercury" he said. I nodded and set the bottle back down. I looked at the pile on the floor and thought about my bag of clothes and ammunition, bedroll and guns. I'd need to carry some food also. I began to wonder how much I could carry on Archie. Tim read my mind. "I've got an extra pack horse down at the corral" he told me. "He's not much to look at, but he can do what you need and I could let you have him cheap. $75."

"OK. I'll take him." I hesitated, considering whether or not I wanted to ask Tim my next questions. As it was, nobody knew where I was going and I liked it that way. On the other hand, I didn't know much about the area where I planned to mine for gold. Tim watched me, saying nothing. Finally I asked what he knew about the Sangre de Cristo Mountains, just north of us, where I had passed through on my way to Cimarron and now planned to return.

Tim sat down on a stool in the shop. "I thought you might be headed there." He fished around in a drawer, pulled out a map, and tossed it to me. "This might help some" he said. I glanced at it. It marked the ranges, a few rivers, and some trails. I put it in my pocket. "I'd try the western slope, if I were you" Tim said. "There's been some gold found there. Don't be surprised if you run into a few others in the area. You may want to join up with a few others, or you may want to do it your own way. One way you have more protection from the Jicarilla Apaches, but you have to trust a stranger or two if you find something." I nodded, filing that away in my mind. "There's been a rumor of a ledge running through the length of the mountains, but I wouldn't put too much stock in that. Oh, one other thing. If you have some gold and need to leave some behind while you haul some out, be sure to leave yourself some kind of trail. A couple guys have left part of their stake behind, then never could find it again when they went back."

I thanked him, gathered up the goods he had on the floor and followed Tim down to the corral. I gave Archie a pat or two as we walked past, and then looked at Tim's pack horse. He was small, kind of a mouse-colored gray, and I thought he looked at me rather balefully as I walked up to him. I patted him a few times and he ignored me completely. I circled a couple times and looked at him a little doubtfully. "Well, I said," you were right when you said he isn't much to look at." Tim grinned a little, but then gestured toward the horse. "He'll do everything you need" he said. He'll go all day long. He comes from mustang stock. He doesn't need a lot of food. You don't need him to win a beauty contest. He just needs to pack your stuff and he can do that." Finally I took Tim's word for it and paid the $75. Tim stuffed the money in his pocket and headed back for his store. "See you in Denver" he called. I waved, and then turned back around. "Hey. What do you call him?" "I call him Fred" Tim called back. "Call him whatever you want. I don't think he's too particular."

"Fred" I muttered under my breath as I loaded the supplies on him. Fred didn't seem to mind, so I tied a rope on him and led him over to Archie. I loaded my bag and bedroll on Archie, put the Winchester in the scabbard, climbed aboard, turned out of the corral and headed north toward the mountains. For the second time in my life, I was leaving Cimarron against my will. I wondered how many times I would find myself starting life over before I was done.

Chapter Ten

I pushed north into the hills, holding west of Raton and pushing into Colorado before the sun was very high overhead. It was my second day on the trail. Late June wasn't a bad time to be moving into the Sangre de Cristo Mountains, but I could see the snow still on the peaks above me. I pulled my jacket tighter around my shoulders and enjoyed the feel of the sun on my shoulders. Archie moved along the trail, probably glad for the chance to get out of the corral. I had a rope tied to Fred, and he carried the mining gear and my bags.

I thought about the situation I had left behind me in Cimarron. I thought the sheriff was being a little optimistic about the idea that the Carson brothers wouldn't go after Jim and Kate after the death of Yates. True, they hadn't killed him—I did that, but Kate was very much involved in what happened. If they had been exposed as cattle rustlers, they might do some pretty drastic things to cover their tracks. I could understand the sheriff wanting to keep the peace, but the remaining Carson brothers might not let that happen. And what about Red? Where was he, and how deep was he in this situation? Even if the sheriff was willing to help Jim and Kate, they might find themselves outgunned. I found myself twisting uneasily in the saddle, not happy with my decision to leave Cimarron, but I couldn't see what other choice I'd had.

I stopped to water the horses at a stream and glanced around at the increasingly thick stands of bristlecone pines and spruce trees as the horses drank. It was a beautiful countryside around me, but I reminded myself that I needed to be aware of dangers besides the Apaches. There were mountain lions in the area, and although I knew they feed mainly on deer, I didn't want to come up on one unexpectedly. And speaking of deer, I was counting on venison as a primary source of food on this trip, but I knew I had to be careful about announcing my presence with a rifle shot. Maybe if I came upon a deer before reaching my destination, it would be good to kill and dress it, then pack it in on Fred. There was always something to keep in mind when you were on your own out here.

I decided to pull off into a small clearing and have something to eat. The sun still felt good on my shoulders as I leaned up against a rock and ate some jerky. I thought about some things Tim had told me concerning mining in the Sangre de Cristo Mountains. He'd said there were some miners working on the western slopes, and I should decide whether I wanted some safety in numbers, or whether I wanted to be a lone wolf and work on my own. I'd not had much luck trusting total strangers before, and where gold was involved, I'd decided that went double. I would trust no one else and work on my own.

Concerning the rumors of a ledge of gold running the length of the mountains, I put little stock in that one. There were people who stood to profit just from gold miners showing up the area, whether or not any gold was found. There were the restaurants and hotels in the bigger cities, liveries selling horses and places selling supplies. Not to mention the thieves who were happy to relieve any would-be miners of their savings before they ever made it out to the gold fields. I decided to discount that rumor altogether and work the western slopes.

Tim had also told me a story about miners showing up with gold "float", as they called it. It seems they were talking about gold ore lying on the surface of the western foothills of the Sangre de Cristo. I wasn't inclined to believe that one either, but Tim seemed to think it was true in some cases, and said the ore had proved to be very rich. I leaned back a little farther and pulled my hat down over my eyes. Well, I needed to have my senses about me and be checking the ground for tracks, if nothing else. I might as well keep an eye out for gold "float", if such a thing really existed.

There was one last tip Tim had given me, which I figured was probably by far the most valuable one. He'd advised on what to look for when choosing an area to begin mining. He told me to look for reddish-purple colored soil in the area, and formations that showed a lot of quartz. I'd decided that was what I'd be looking for. I wondered idly for a moment why Tim didn't go mining for the gold himself, since he seemed to know so much about it. I finally decided that it just wasn't in his nature to take the chances. If there were good strikes in the Colorado Mountains and Tim had a successful mining store in Denver, he could make plenty of money without risking his neck out here. Takes all kinds, and I wasn't sure but what Tim was the smart one. I sighed and got up, climbing back on Archie and heading north again. I wanted to make camp close to the pass I'd decided to go over to get to the western slopes. I didn't want to camp out in the snow, which Tim had assured was still there on the pass. I pulled out my map and took a look. Sangre de Cristo pass was what it said on the map. I didn't much care what they called it if I could pass over and get to the western slopes. I headed Archie north, gave Fred a tug to follow along, and started back out.

… Sam polished the bar absently while watching the two men who had come into his saloon. They were drifters, by the look of them, and he expected they would just pass on through town. It was the fragment of conversation he'd picked up when he delivered their beer that had gotten his attention. He'd picked up the name Carson. When he'd hesitated after setting the bottles down, they'd buttoned up and stopped talking. He polished some more and watched from the corner of his eyes while they lowered the levels on the beer. After a while, he motioned his nephew Mike to come over. He gestured toward the table with the two drifters. "Go over and see if they want another beer. If you hear any of their conversation, I want to know about it." Mike looked at him quizzically. Sam shrugged. "Just do it" he advised. "I especially want to know if you hear any names. Don't come back and talk to me until you're done serving them."

Mike nodded and walked over to the table. Sam turned and walked to the end of the bar, watching the reflection in the saloon window as Mike walked over and talked to the strangers. He returned, picked up two more bottles of beer and carried them back to the table. After he had left the beer, taken their money, and come back to the register, Sam walked over to him. "Well?" he asked. Mike put the money in the register, then turned his back on the center of the saloon as he answered. "I couldn't make much of the conversation. Maybe a few names, though." Sam waited. "One name sounded like

Red, and the other might have been Santos. Plus they mentioned the two remaining Carson brothers."

Sam stared at the bar and let that one sink in. It sounded like the worst possible news. He'd half expected that Red would come back to see the other two Carson brothers. Red probably liked stealing money better than earning it, and the setup for cattle rustling with the Carsons had been too good to leave. The name Santos was also a concern. He was known in the territory as a small time gunfighter, probably bigger in his own mind than anyone else's, but he wouldn't object to bushwhacking a man, as Red had tried to do. That made him dangerous. Sam absently served another whiskey at the bar and considered his options. They would find out soon enough that Chance had left the area. Sam still disagreed with that decision by the sheriff. Certain people would never make the peace lawfully and willfully, and the Carson brothers were among those, especially after their brother died. Better to face them and have it out now than wait for them to pick the time and place... too late for that.

Sam considered a few avenues in his mind while he picked up some dirty glasses and carried them back over to the bar. He thought about paying a visit to Sheriff Stanton, but dismissed that almost immediately. The sheriff wouldn't move unless there was an imminent danger to the peace in the town. At the least, he needed to pay a visit to the Randolphs and let them know the other two Carsons were back in town. It would have to be in the morning. He didn't have enough light to find his way tonight.

... I rode on to the north, lifting my jacket collar against the chill and noting how the trail was now rising up into more mountainous country. I'd made good progress throughout the afternoon, and if I was reading my map correctly, was close to finding a place to camp for the night. I wanted to be through the Sangre de Cristo Pass and down out of snow country tomorrow, if that was at all possible.

Archie seemed to follow the trail without much guidance from me, and Fred seemed happy enough to follow along behind us. There were cliff walls rising up now on my right. In the setting sun, the rocks seemed to glow a deep maroon color. I wondered idly what would cause that red color. Tim could probably tell me, if I remembered to ask. We came around a corner that offered a surprisingly good view for quite a ways ahead of me, before the trail veered to the left. I scanned the country ahead, sizing it up for a camping spot off the trail. I heard a slight rumbling noise and looked overhead, wondering where the thunder was coming from. The sky was cloudless, and I frowned in confusion. A couple hundred yards ahead, a bit of dust and some small rocks began to tumble across the trail. Landslide! I sprang into action as soon as the word formed in my mind.

I wheeled Archie and went back the way I'd come, swinging Fred around as we went and pulling him after us. There was an overhang on the trail about fifty yards back, and I would have to hope there was enough shelter. I was dismounting as I rode Archie in, and I grabbed a halter in each hand, pulling all of us under the overhang. I looped Archie's lead rope around one hand and lifted the collar of my jacket to cover my mouth. Up ahead, the rumbling sound was now growing extremely loud. Larger and larger rocks began to bounce across the path, until there were boulders crashing across, tearing through the underbrush below and uprooting small trees in their path. The slide area seemed to be building back toward us slowly. I didn't have many illusions at this point that the overhang could hold up to those boulders. I could only hope we were, as a result of pure dumb luck, far enough back. I pulled the horses close and talked as soothingly as I could. Archie was surprisingly calm, but Fred was skittish and trembling. That made two of us.

The noise seemed deafening at this point, and the dust was almost chokingly thick. I concentrated on breathing through my jacket and hoped the horses could hold up to it. The dust was so thick it was difficult to see anything, but I glanced up once in a while to see what I could. There seemed to still be some room between us and the edge of the slide, and I could only hope it wouldn't extend this far. I stood for some time with my head down, jacket pulled across my mouth and nose, and my eyes closed. I decided that if one or more of those boulders was headed for us, I didn't need to see it. After some time, it seemed that the noise level was decidedly less than before. Finally I looked up at the path in front of me. The dust still hung very thick in the air, and while there were still rocks, tree branches and debris falling across the path, I didn't see the huge boulders any more. While I watched, in a surprisingly short period of time, the noise dropped away and the slide seemed to stop.

I continued to soothe the horses, then splashed some water from my canteen onto an old pair of socks and used them to help clear their nostrils. I spoke soothingly and continued to pat them until the fear seemed to leave them. When that was done, I looked at the trail ahead of me and took stock of our situation.

It seemed to me there were really only two choices—I could keep moving ahead and look for a place to sleep for the night, or I could stay where I was and do the same. I thought about the landslide we had just come through and the possibility of some unstable rocks still up on those mountains after the slide, and opted for choice number two. I walked Archie and Fred back down the path for a couple hundred yards, then located a spot under some trees back off the trail a bit. I decided I could get happy with that as a spot to sleep tonight.

After tying Archie and Fred to a couple of limbs, I stripped off their saddles and rubbed them down as best I could with an old rag. I decided to camp without a fire and made do for dinner with some more jerky and some cold beans. After that I pulled together some pine needles and laid my bedroll across them. It had been more adventure than I wanted today, but I was still alive. That certainly counted for something. I closed my eyes and drifted off to sleep.

I eased Archie down the steep winding path, with Sangre de Cristo pass behind me, for which I was thankful. I had made camp after the landslide, and then got an early start to put the pass behind me and get far enough down the mountain to camp out of the snow. I'd managed to do that, but last night had been colder than I'd bargained for. The morning sun was beginning to thaw me a little. Archie picked his way carefully down the trail and I gave him his head. He might be glad for a warmer camping spot too.

After we had descended a little farther I found a trail and struck that one back to the north. I kept one wary eye out for both Apaches and other miners. I had in mind a spot I was looking for to set up operations, I just didn't know if I could find something to fit the bill. The map I had from Tim showed the Rio Grande River winding through the area, hopefully just north of where I was now and there appeared to be several tributaries feeding into it. It would be a convenient source of fresh water if I could find a cave on a hillside near one of those tributaries. I didn't want to be right on the water—too much chance of running into someone else. A dugout area or cave near some promising mountainsides or cave walls with rich quartz formations and close to the water. Now that was what I needed.

We struck a stream I hoped was one of those tributaries and followed it north for a couple hours. The sun was getting pretty much high overhead when the sound of more water told me we may have reached the Rio Grande. I held the horses back under the trees and watched the water flowing by me, checking my map and feeling pretty sure we had found the Rio Grande. After a while I worked on to the west watching for a place to ford the river. After we had crossed over we doubled back a little to the east until I found another tributary and we followed that one north again. As we neared time to find a camping spot, there appeared to be some good quartz formations on the mountain walls, glowing a little red in the setting sun.

Finally I saw what looked like a small recess or overhang on the side of the mountain and I pulled the horses over and climbed to the spot I'd seen. There was a small overhang and an opening beyond. I tied off the horses and stepped into the opening, following it into a small cave. I explored it briefly. The back of the cave narrowed into a farther opening. I followed that through and found an additional small room at the back of the cave. This one appeared to be enclosed on all sides, with one small opening in the ceiling. With any luck that would open to woods and underbrush above, allowing the smoke from a small fire to escape undetected. I was delighted with what I'd found. The back wall was too dark to see clearly, so I struck a match and my jaw dropped. There were two balls of what appeared to be roughly processed gold ore.

Chapter 11

Sam stopped halfway through his morning bar cleaning routine and motioned for Mike to come back over. "Can you cover for me this morning? I should be back before it gets too busy." Mike nodded. "Good." Sam slapped him on the shoulder and headed toward the back door. He stopped off in the storage room. He started to pick up his shotgun, thought better of it and picked up Red's old rifle instead, along with a box of ammunition. "I'll be at the Randolph's place if you need me," he tossed over his shoulder, and then he was gone through the back door.

As Sam walked down the main street on his way to the livery stable, he passed the Cimarron jail and saw a light inside. He hesitated, wondering whether he should talk to Sheriff Stanton. He couldn't really fault the sheriff for moving Chance Reilly on down the road in hopes of preserving the peace. But the nagging thought stayed with him that maybe at this point in his life the sheriff just didn't have the stomach to take on the Carsons. Sam stood for several seconds, then finally walked over to the jail and pushed through the front door. Sheriff Stanton looked up as Sam came in, his face registering surprise when he saw the rifle.

"I'm headed out to the Randolph's place" Sam announced without delay. "There were a couple drifters in the saloon last night, and we heard the names Red and Santos. I think Jim and Kate might be in for some trouble." Stanton studied Sam's face, and in the light Sam saw how tired the sheriff looked. "I have some things I have to do here today" Stanton said eventually. "I'll be out there one day this week, or you can come back for me tonight if you need me." Sam stood unmoving for a while, thinking that timetable might be too late, but the sheriff seemed to have made up his mind. Finally, Sam just nodded and headed for the door. At the livery stable, he saddled his horse and started for the Randolph place.

The morning sunshine and gentle mountain breeze did little to lift Sam's spirits as he rode toward the Randolph spread. He conceded that the sheriff might be right about the urgency of the situation. Just because he'd heard the Carson name in the bar didn't mean they were planning an immediate strike. Chances were, though, that word had reached them about their brother. That meant trouble, and Sam wasn't a man who liked to take chances about when trouble might come. He'd always been one to face it immediately when he could. The future of this whole territory depended on having more people like the Randolphs and fewer people like the Carson brothers.

Jim Randolph was out working with a horse in the corral when Sam rode into the yard. If Randolph was surprised, his expression didn't show it. He tied off the horse, removed his gloves, and walked over to shake hands with Sam. "What brings you this way?" he asked.

Sam swung down. "I wish I had a more cheerful reason" he began. Jim nodded. "Come on into the house. I'm sure we have some coffee for you."

Sam trailed behind Randolph into the kitchen of the ranch house. Kate glanced up curiously when they came in. She brought some coffee and home baked bread to the table, then sat down with them. Sam took a minute to gather his thoughts, and then began: "So, we had a couple drifters in the saloon last night. Never saw them before and they didn't seem to know anybody. They pretty much kept to themselves. I managed to pick bits and pieces of their conversation. They were talking about Jack and Caleb Carson. No mention of the youngest one. I'm assuming' they know he's dead. They also talked about Red and a gun hand name Santos. This could be pretty bad." Sam paused and looked at the Randolphs. Both of them sat without much expression, but they were very much listening to him.

Sam paused, and then continued. "You know they aren't going to leave this alone. I stopped off to talk to Sheriff Stanton this morning, but he isn't ready to get involved in this. If you ask me, he won't get into it until it's too late. I came to tell you two things: One, you need to be on the lookout all the time. And two, you can count on my help. You just tell me what you need." Jim passed his hand quickly over his face. "Out here, a man kinda has to deal with his troubles himself," he began. Sam interrupted. "Sometimes, a man needs a neighbor to help out. You're good people and I'm here to help. I won't take no for an answer." Jim paused, glanced up at Sam, and nodded. Kate smiled and reached out to pat his hand. "You know how much danger you could be in?" asked Jim. Sam nodded.

Jim Randolph reached his hand across the table and they shook. "My nephew Mike might want in on this too" Sam said. "I'm only sorry the sheriff ran Chance Reilly out of here. If enough good folks come together, sometimes we can stop the bad." Out of the corner of his eye, Sam saw Kate's eyes drop to the table when he mentioned Chance Reilly. After a moment, she went over to a smaller table in the kitchen, pulled out a pen and some paper, and began writing. Sam's eyes returned to Jim Randolph. "I know a thing or two about setting up a defensive perimeter" he said. "I thought I'd forget everything about the army and that war between the states, but maybe there's a couple good things to remember. If you want to go outside I'll help you take a look around and make a plan in case we need it." Jim pushed back his chair and led the way to the door. When Sam looked back, Kate was busy writing.

Sam and Jim stepped out to the yard and looked around. Sam motioned toward the bunkhouse, some fifty yards away from the ranch house. "There's your first line of defense" Sam said. You can meet them first from there. He glanced around the yard. "There's some cover on the porch, and of course from the windows of the house..." He paused, thinking. "You need someplace to fall back to and still have a good defensive position without retreating all the way into the house." His eyes fell on a large woodpile, about halfway between the bunkhouse and the main house. He began rolling up his sleeves and walking to the woodpile. "Just what we need" he said.

Kate had started her letter, then stopped and second guessed herself. She held the sheet of paper with the address Chance had given her in one hand and the pen in the other. Was it too soon to ask for his help? Would he even get the letter in time? Was it fair to ask him to come back to town and deal with the brothers of the man he had killed? She stared at the wall in front of her and thought. A very short period of time had crystalized things in her mind about the death of Yates. She had talked to her father several times and he had told her repeatedly there'd been no other way. This morning's conversation with Sam only underscored that. She glanced down at the paper and began writing again.

Jim and Sam finished splitting the woodpile in two. They had moved the original back a short way to create a direct fallback from the bunkhouse. The second pile they had created on the other side of the ranch house, tucked down a bit around the corner. Sam hoped it could serve as a surprise if anyone rushed the house. Sweat ran down his cheeks and neck as they finished stacking the wood. He glanced over at Jim. "Anything else we need to be concerned about? They're not above ambush, you know. Is there any place you're at regularly where you'd be out in the open?" Jim considered that one, glancing around the lower pasture, then up toward the upper pasture. "I better show you a place where I suspect they've been cutting the fence and stealing cattle" he said at length.

When they arrived at the upper pasture and dismounted, Sam ran his hand along the barbed wire and noted the places where it had been cut and wound back together. "Well," he said eventually, "I think you're right about the cattle rustling happening here." His eyes measured the Carson pasture in front of him, with trees bordering the pasture on the far side. His glance dropped behind him, across the open pasture of the Randolph place, finally ending where the cliffs formed a natural barrier at the far side. He turned to survey the pasture and trees immediately below them. A natural stand of timber formed the border at the south side of the pasture, and afforded a field of fire into the Carson property. "I'd not be coming up here to check the wire any more by yourself" he said abruptly. "If I'm here I'll give you cover from the trees down there." He thought for a moment. "If I'm not here, can Kate handle a rifle well enough to cover you?" Jim nodded immediately. "I taught her how to handle a rifle myself. She's good with it." Sam smiled and nodded. He glanced around one more time. "One more thing" he said. "When you're up here at this fence, try to keep your horse between you and the Carson pasture." They remounted and headed back to the house.

Kate finished her letter as she heard her father and Sam returning. She folded the letter, put it in the envelope and wrote down the Denver address. She sealed the envelope and went out through the back door to join the men. Sam and Jim shook hands one more time, and Sam swung up on his horse. Kate hurried across the yard, calling his name. Sam paused and swung his horse around to meet her. "Sam," she said, "I can't thank you enough for your help. Can I ask you for just one more small favor?" "You just name it" Sam replied. Kate extended the letter. Sam reached down, took the letter, and his eyes registered the name on the envelope. A small smile touched his lips, then he grinned broadly and tucked the letter into his shirt pocket. "My pleasure" he said, and then he spurred his horse out of the yard.

… I squatted on my heels in the cave, staring at the balls of gold ore. I looked around me carefully several times, then finally walked over to pick up one of the balls. I was surprised at the weight. I hefted it in my hands a few times, then set it down and lifted the other one. It was approximately the same size and weight. I remained on my heels, looked around me one more time, and considered the possibilities. This cave had obviously been used before by a miner or miners. There were no signs of anyone having lived here recently, which was a little puzzling. If they had been attacked by the Apaches here, there would surely be some spent shells around. If they had been surprised and attacked while they were out mining, why would the cave be so completely empty? I thought back to Tim's story about miners who were unable to find their campsites again after hauling some of their gold out of the hills. That seemed the most likely possibility.

I thought for a while about whether I wanted to camp in this same site, and whether or not I could consider those gold balls to be mine. I decided eventually that the answer to both questions was yes. This was such an ideal site; I would take my chances on the original occupants returning. If they hadn't made their way back for those gold balls, it didn't seem likely they were coming. If they did return, they could certainly have the gold they had mined and processed. That had led to my second question: if they didn't return by the time I was ready to leave, was that gold mine to keep? I decided that it was unlikely they would be coming back if they hadn't already, and there was no sense in leaving the gold in the cave where it would do nobody any good.

I went back outside and began bringing my clothes and equipment inside. I decided right away I would sleep in the back room of the cave. It felt safer back there, and a short exploration and experiment taught me I could build a small fire back there and let the smoke drift out through the small opening at the back. The smoke seemed to filter out through the small trees above ground, and seemed pretty well concealed. I didn't plan to build any fires during daylight, in any case. I hauled my bedroll, blankets and clothes to the back, along with what food I had and a couple of cooking pots. I'd be needing to bring in a little firewood this afternoon or in the morning, and I also needed to shoot a deer for some food. I was close enough to the river to walk down there for a drink. I carried the mining equipment to the front of the cave.

With that done, I stripped the saddles from Archie and Fred, rubbed them down, and picketed them near the mouth of the cave. They could provide a little warning if someone was nearing the entrance. I then took my rifle down near the stream, crouched behind some small trees and underbrush, and waited to see if I would see any deer coming down for a drink. With dusk approaching, a small herd of four came down to the water. I shot a small buck, dressed him, and hauled the meat back up to the cave.

That night, wrapped up in my bedroll, I stared up at the ceiling of the cave and considered the good luck I'd had so far on this trip. Well, other than the landslide. You couldn't really call that good luck. That aside, I'd reached a place that appeared to have good mining possibilities. I had a big head start on the amount of gold I'd need to mine. This cave felt warm and safe, especially after the landslide and the frigid nights I'd spent near the snow line. I would need some more luck I knew, in terms of mining and processing the gold, and especially in staying away from the Jicarilla warriors. I'd keep my head down, and I would put safety over the gold every time. With that thought in mind, I drifted off to sleep.

Morning found me leading Fred up a rocky path along the face of the mountains. I saw a number of places where there were quartz veins along the face of the rock, and I could see some specks of gold in them as I studied a few. In each case, though, I felt I was too far out and in the open to do any work. Safety remained my number one priority, and I stopped to check my back trail often. So far I seemed to be alone up here. By midday I had eliminated every prospective site I had seen, and was becoming a bit discouraged. I stopped for some beef jerky and water and let Fred graze a few patches of mountain grass I found in a high meadow. After I finished eating, I made my decision and stood up. I would concentrate on finding a few caves where I might be able to prospect.

I led Fred a little off the path, scrambling up some slippery patches of shale and loose rock, pausing to let Fred pick his way when he was hesitant to follow. I stopped to memorize some landmarks as I went, and knew I needed to leave well before dark in order to find my way back. I checked a few small caves, looking carefully for any sign of mountain lions or bears before going in. The third cave I checked seemed to have some possibilities. There were a couple streaks of quartz flecked with gold extending back into the cave. The area toward the entrance had enough light to work without candles. Going farther back, I could see I would need candlelight to do my work when I went deeper. I made a note to put a few candles in the saddle bags tomorrow.

Before I left I took out my pocketknife and pried loose some of the rock from the quartz vein. I held some in my hands to examine it, then walked back to get my pick. I took several swings, surprised at the amount of exertion it took to knock down a decent sample of ore. I picked some up, sifted out the dirt and rock as best I could, and kept a few larger chunks flecked with gold. I took those over and put them in the saddle bags. It occurred to me that I should bring the box with mesh with me tomorrow. Sifting through the material one time before I hauled it back to the cave would save hauling a lot of dirt and rock. I patted Fred on the neck. "You'll thank me tomorrow" I told him.

I led Fred out of the cave and down the rocky slope we'd come up, checking my landmarks and memorizing the terrain as best I could. With the two balls of gold ore I'd found, maybe this cave and one or two in the surrounding area would give me all I'd need for a start at ranching. I worked my way back to my home cave and tethered Fred next to Archie. I checked around as I entered the cave. It seemed to be undisturbed since I'd left this morning. I settled in for the evening and felt I had established what my routine would be until I had enough gold ore to pull out. Maybe after the next few days I would have a better idea how long it would take.

Chapter Twelve

Kate crossed the ranch yard to draw a bucket of water from the well. Her instinct by now was to scan the lower pasture and bunkhouse area for any sign of activity, and she did so now as she pumped the water. There was no sign of activity. It had been over two weeks since Sam had come to see them and she had sent the letter to Chance with Sam. The threat of attack from the Carson brothers accompanied by the strange silence and lack of any visible threat had worn on her, and she was even more concerned about her father. She finished pumping the water, and with another glance around the ranch yard carried the bucket back to the kitchen.

She knew that for a while her father had followed Sam's advice about not checking the upper pasture unless both of them went, but now he complained from time to time about all the precautions he was taking and how much less work he was getting done because of them. She worried that he would let down his guard and be ambushed by the Carsons. She heated the bucket of water over the stove, poured it into the kitchen sink and began to wash some dishes, watching her father through the window as she did so. He was in the corral, putting new shoes on the buckskin horse that he rode most often. His rifle lay against the rails of the corral as he worked. Kate turned and went over to the table to carry the breakfast dishes to the sink. As she placed them in the dishwater she glanced back through the window, just in time to see her father finish saddling the buckskin. He grabbed his rifle and swung on his horse, leaving the corral and heading toward the upper pasture.

Kate watched for a moment, and then knew instinctively where he was headed. She had suspected for a few days that he was going to the upper pasture to check the fence for any signs of rustling, and she was sure that was where he was headed now. She dried her hands quickly, grabbed her rifle from the rack by the back door, and ran out to the corral. She saddled her mare and kicked the mare into a gallop toward the upper pasture. She intended to give him cover whether he knew about it or not.

Sam moved around behind the counter of the bar, hoping he was giving the appearance of being busy. He washed a couple of glasses that were already as clean as they were going to get, and moved a few bottles of whiskey from one place to another. Mike glanced at him quizzically, and Sam simply shook his head. Mike hadn't been here long enough to recognize either of the remaining Carson brothers, but Sam knew it was Caleb Carson sitting with another man at a window table across the room. He considered his options. The extent of his friendship with Jim and Kate Randolph probably wasn't known to the Carson brothers, so they felt safe enough coming to his saloon. The man sitting with Caleb Carson wasn't known to him, but he wore a tied down gun and had a certain arrogance about him. Sam thought it likely he was Santos. It was also likely that Jack Carson and possibly Red were in the area somewhere. That would make four men against Jim and Kate, they probably didn't know the Carsons were back in town. Sam thought again about walking over to Sherriff Stanton's office, then decided against it. He'd already pretty much let it be known that he wouldn't take action unless or until hostilities had started.

A movement from the table near the window caught Sam's eye, and he saw Caleb Carson motioning toward him. Sam picked up a bottle of whiskey and walked over to the table. Carson and the other man both indicated their empty glasses, and Sam filled them up. Caleb Carson tossed down his drink, slammed the glass down, and motioned again. Sam filled it back up and waited. Carson circled a finger around the top of his glass, seemed to consider a couple questions, then took the direct approach: "You have someone named Chance Reilly working here?" Sam shrugged, then set the whiskey bottle down on the table. "Did have. He pulled out and left a few weeks ago. No notice, nothing. Had to get my nephew Mike over there to move down from Denver and help me out." He jerked a thumb in the direction of the bar. Carson glanced over toward the bar, nodded absently, then reached in his pocket for a gold coin, which he slapped down on the table in payment for the whiskey. He refilled his glass and paid no further attention to Sam.

Sam returned to the bar and allowed fifteen minutes to pass by. Carson and Santos, if that's who it was, seemed in no hurry and paid no further attention to Sam. After the fifteen minutes had passed, Sam tapped Mike on the shoulder. "You know the drill. Cover for me. I'm headed out to the Randolph place." Mike simply nodded, and Sam thought for a second longer. "Find some excuse to close the place down a little early, and then come out to the Randolph's yourself. Come armed and be careful." Mike nodded again. Sam move to the back storage room and pulled out his spare shotgun and a box of ammunition. After a moment's hesitation, he also picked up the rifle he had taken from Red and another box of ammunition. He shoved the ammunition in his pockets, ducked out through the back door, saddled up his horse and headed north toward the Randolph ranch.

It was late afternoon when Sam reached the Randolph ranch yard. He noticed that both Jim's horse and Kate's were missing from the corral. Sam walked over to the ranch house and knocked on the front door. When he got no answer, he walked around to the back and knocked on the kitchen door. Still getting no answer, he tried the door and walked in. He called out a time or two and got no answer. He walked back out the kitchen door onto the porch, put his hand up to shield his eyes and stared out toward the lower pasture. Remembering his conversation with Jim about the suspected cattle rustling taking place in the upper pasture, Sam began walking back to his horse, casting one eye toward the bunkhouse as he walked. It appeared to be empty. Halfway back to his horse, Sam heard a rifle shot coming from the direction of the upper pasture. Quickening his pace, Sam climbed aboard his horse, removed Red's rifle from the scabbard, and spurred his horse toward the upper pasture.

Kate saw with relief that her father was dismounted in the upper pasture, examining the wire partway along the fence, unharmed and with no one else in sight. She resisted her first impulse to ride out toward him, remembering instead Sam's advice to give cover from under the trees to the south of where Jim stood. She guided her horse in that direction, keeping to the tree line as she went. When she reached an area providing good cover under the trees, she dismounted and hitched her horse to a low-lying tree limb. She pulled her rifle from the saddle and lay down behind a fallen log, glancing over at her father while she did so. She was relieved to see that he had at least kept part of Sam's advice in mind, because he seemed to be keeping his horse between himself and the Carson pasture in front of him. When the first shot rang out from the trees on the far side of the Carson pasture, it came as a complete shock.

Kate saw her father falling to the ground, his legs sliding out from underneath him as he fell. He grabbed his left leg and she could hear his shout from where she lay. Shocked, she had the presence of mind to sight her rifle across the pasture. When she heard a second and third shot and saw a puff of smoke, she returned fire. After a couple of shots, she risked a glance back toward her father. She saw that he had managed to grab the reins, and using both hands and all his weight, had pulled his horse to the ground in front of him. Feeling relief wash over her as she realized he now had cover, she turned and continued to fire shots into the trees and brush where she had first seen the smoke.

Jim Randolph lay on the ground, feeling a stabbing pain coming from his left leg. He could see the blood oozing onto his pant leg, and through the shock came the realization that he had been ambushed from the Carson side. He'd had the presence of mind to pull his horse down as cover. He was pretty sure that the second and third shots had killed the horse. He didn't dare raise his head over the level of the saddle, but he was able to pull his rifle from the saddle, lay it over the horse and return fire in the direction of the shots fired at him. He began to realize that shots were also being fired from the woods to his right and he knew that Kate had come to his aid. He hung on grimly, straining to retain consciousness. He managed to pump several more shots towards the Carson land.

Sam entered the upper pasture at full gallop, leaning low over the saddle to shield himself from the Carson's gunshots and allowing the fire from Kate and Jim to serve as cover. He held to the tree line and guided his horse to the right of Kate. When he reached a spot about thirty yards to her right, he yanked the rifle from the scabbard and dove behind a boulder. With Jim on the left and Kate on the right, he formed the third point of a bracket around the shooters. No matter how good their cover, they were going to feel uncomfortable now, he reflected grimly. Using Red's repeating rifle, and feeling silently thankful that he had grabbed three boxes of ammunition, he lay down a heavy line of fire into the trees where he could see their smoke. Pausing for a moment to look carefully into the trees, he thought he could see a patch of red among the green of the leaves and brown of the tree trunks. He laid his sights on the patch of red and exhaled slowly as he squeezed the trigger. The patch of red disappeared. He knew he had probably done no more than graze someone's back, but a bullet wound stung all the same. When he saw and heard movement in the brush or twigs, he aimed a shot at the movement. After a few more minutes, they could hear no more shots coming from across the pasture.

Knowing that Jim Randolph had stopped firing earlier, Sam called out softly: "Kate" he said, "I think they're pulling back. We need to get your father back to the house, so let's let them go." He heard a faint "OK" coming from Kate's position. Sam waited for five minutes, and then began walking his horse to Kate's position. He found her prone behind a fallen log, rifle still at the ready across the log. "I think they're gone" Sam told her. "If you can stay here for a few minutes longer to give me cover, I'm going over to check on Jim." Kate nodded her agreement, the strain and worry showing in her face when she glanced across toward her father. Sam walked his horse across the pasture, following his own advice by keeping the horse between him and the Carson pasture. When he reached Jim Randolph, he found him unconscious. A quick check showed a strong pulse, and he motioned for Kate to join him.

Finding that Jim's horse was dead, they lifted him to Sam's horse, and Sam swung aboard behind him. Kate, keeping the rifle leveled in the direction of the Carson property, climbed on her horse and they slowly carried Jim back to the ranch house. They found Mike in the yard, having just arrived, and Sam sent him back to town to fetch the doctor. Sam and Kate then carried Jim into the house, setting him down on the sofa. They cut away the pants leg below the wound. It appeared that the bullet had passed through his leg cleanly. Kate washed the wound, and while they waited for Doc Chapman to arrive they discussed the situation. Jim seemed to fall into a fitful sleep on the sofa, moaning softly from time to time as he tossed back and forth.

"They're not done trying to take the ranch, are they?" Kate asked. Sam shook his head. "No, I don't think so. They thought they saw an easy way to take Jim out of the picture, leaving only you, and they probably know they at least wounded him. They probably also figured out there were two guns returning fire, and decided to pull back and find better odds if they can." Sam produced a toothpick from his pocket and began to chew it while he thought things over for a while longer. "They have the advantage because we don't know how many of them there are" he continued after a while. "I know we can figure on the two living Carson brothers and we can just go ahead and figure that Red is with them too. And I'm pretty sure there's another low-life named Santos who has thrown in with them." He stared at the table while he talked, lifting his gaze once in a while out the window to the ranch yard. The sun was beginning to set, casting shadows over the bunkhouse and corral. Sam thought for a while longer. "They could have some additional help coming by now. People like the Carsons don't like a fair fight."

Kate absorbed that piece of information, walked over to check briefly on her father, then returned to sit at the table with Sam, who was now silent and concentrating his attention out the window. "What can we do?" she asked simply. Sam pulled his gaze back to her, removed the toothpick and thought for a while before answering. "We'll have to see what shape your Dad is in," he answered "before we'll know if he can at least use a rifle from cover on the porch." He looked around at the defensive positions they had created in the yard using the firewood. Now he swung back around to look at Kate as he talked. "We can get in touch with Sheriff Stanton to help us now. I hope he doesn't have any ideas about talking sense into the Carsons. This is a range war and he needs to treat it like one." He walked over to the window, and then came back to the table. "One thing we have going for us," he finished. "They don't know about Mike. He'll be here to help us, and they don't know about that extra gun."

Kate covered Sam's hand with hers on the table. "Thank you" she said simply. The corners of Sam's mouth formed a smile around the toothpick. "Wouldn't miss it for anything" he said. "One good thing about getting older. It gets easier to sort out the good guys and the bad guys. Decisions come a little easier." With that he picked up his rifle and moved out to the porch, sitting in the lengthening shadows and keeping the rifle trained on the approaches to the house.

Darkness had settled in when approaching hoof beats signaled the arrival of Doc Chapman with Mike. The doctor came in and examined the wound. Jim had awakened and was pale but alert, grimacing occasionally as Doc Chapman probed around the entrance and the exit wound. Eventually he straightened up with a small smile. "Good news, Jim" he announced. "I know it don't feel too good right now, but that's a clean wound. I don't need to set it, because the leg ain't broke. You might feel it every now and then when a storm is comin', but you'll be walking just fine after a while." With that, he threw a few instruments back in his bag and let himself out the back door.

 Mike leaned against the wall near the kitchen, hat in his hands. He had spoken very little since arriving, and glanced quizzically at Sam after the doctor was gone. Sam walked over and placed a hand on his shoulder. "Still prepared to help out?" he asked. Mike nodded. Sam walked him over to the door. "I need you to get back to town tonight and let Sheriff Stanton know what happened. Tell him exactly what went down, that it was an ambush, plain and simple. Then make sure the saloon is boarded up inside. We'll have to shut it down for a while. Be back here by mid-morning if you can. Bring your rifle and plenty of ammo. We got us a shootin' war here, unless I miss my guess." Mike ducked out the back door and they could hear him leaving the yard just a few minutes after the doctor was gone.

Sam poured a glass of whiskey and carried it over to Jim. "Here" he said simply. This will help some with the pain and maybe get you back to sleep. "We're gonna need your help soon if you're able." Jim tossed off the whiskey without a word and settled himself back on the sofa. Kate walked out to the kitchen and began preparing some food. Sam walked in and leaned against a counter. "Here's how I see it" Sam told her. "You and hopefully Jim can be on the porch behind cover come morning. I'll be behind the woodpile near the bunkhouse. My original plan was to set up a first line of defense at the bunkhouse, but the numbers are against us, so we'll pull in closer. When Mike gets here, he'll go behind the other woodpile, but he'll hold fire at first. They don't know to expect him. I think they'll come from the cover of trees over there." He pointed to the area behind the bunkhouse. "I don't know how many guns they have, but it will probably be four, and with any luck they'll think they're coming against only me and you. We can hold them off if they don't have reinforcements." He started to say something else, then seemed to think better of it and lapsed into silence.

Kate nodded and put some food on the table. They ate in silence, hearing only gentle snores from Jim on the sofa. When they were done, Kate asked "What about tonight?" "I'll take first watch on the porch" Sam said. "Can you spell me around 2 o'clock?" Kate nodded and Sam moved toward the porch, picking up his rifle as he went. She had one more question as he left. "Sam?" He turned at the door and looked back at her. "We might have one more gun, if he gets my letter in time and comes. You saw my letter to Chance, right?" A small smile played around Sam's lips. "Oh, he'll come all right. I just hope he gets that letter in time. That would help us a considerable amount." The door made no noise as it closed behind him.

Chapter Thirteen

I squatted on my heels in the center of the cave and contemplated the pile of ore and sediment I'd accumulated over the past few weeks. It was all scooped in a pile in the corner. I'd put off trying to process any of the residue and sediment so far, probably because I didn't really know what to do or how it would come out. Tim had said that three or four crudely processed gold balls might be enough to get me a start on my own place. Trouble was, I wasn't really sure how big those gold balls needed to be or how pure the content needed to be. I was going to have to do some guessing. I already had the two gold balls I'd found when I came in. That left only one or two more, and it was time I found out had much I had sitting over there in the corner.

I sighed, stood up and made myself a little breakfast. I wouldn't do any mining today. It was time to try to process some of the ore. After I'd eaten, I went outside to get some water and food for Archie and Fred. Archie nuzzled me a little, and Fred glared at me as usual. Or maybe it was that bad eye of his. I'm sure I'll never know. I scouted around the cave a little bit, found no tracks or footprints, also as usual, and went back inside.

I went over to where my gear was stored and pulled out a large pan, heavy work gloves, and the bottle of mercury. Then I got out the wire mesh boxes I'd been using to sift out the loose dirt and rock I'd knocked out at the mining site. Finally I took out the mortar and pestle and went to work. I used the mortar and pestle to break up the chunks of quartz and gold. I poured the small bits of rock and residue on the wire mesh before I'd broken them down too far, and saved off the pieces showing good color. Bits that were small enough to have fallen through the mesh but still showed good color I fished out and added to the pile I'd saved off the top of the mesh. I kept feeding the ore from the pile in the corner, taking a break only when my hands couldn't keep up the grinding. I kept going with only a small break for some food, and stepped outside the cave a couple times just to stretch and get some fresh air.

Finally, about mid-afternoon, I'd done all the grinding I could stand to do for the day. Now came the part I felt least sure about. I got out the large pan, dropped a pretty fair amount of the quartz and gold in it, and then poured some mercury on it. It bubbled a bit, and when I stirred the bottom of the pan for a while, I saw purer gold color in the bottom. I gathered it together, packing it into a ball as best I could, then set it aside and compared it to the two balls of gold ore I'd originally found in this cave. They seemed to be pretty similar in color and consistency, though mine was smaller of course. I kept it up for the rest of the day until I had a ball about the size of the other two I had found, and decided that was a good time to stop for the day.

The next morning I evaluated the amount of unprocessed ore I had left, and knew I was well short of another ball. I decided that before I went back to the site I would keep working at it until I had another ball, though I knew it would be smaller. I found that I was getting a little more skilled at the processing, and went back to grinding, sifting, pouring the mercury and packing the gold residue into a ball. A little while after stopping for some lunch, I had a ball about half the size of the other three, and I had processed all the ore and sediment I'd brought back to the cave.

I stepped outside the cave, checking the area around me for footprints or any sign of activity, which by now was an ingrained habit. I sat down and leaned back against the rock wall next to the cave entrance, soaking in a little sunshine and deciding what to do next. Maybe I had enough to get a place like I wanted, and maybe I didn't. I would have to see Tim in Denver to find somebody to assess and buy this gold. Until then I didn't really know how much I had. There was a strong urge in me to quit while I was ahead; the other part of me said to stay a while longer and finish what I started. I found my thoughts drifting back to Kate and Cimarron, but it was too soon to hope for a new start there. The sheriff had said a year before I could come back. At length I stood, went over and got the horses ready for another trip back to the mining site. I would stay at least a while longer.

I followed a trail that by now was familiar, tracing my path to the site where I'd worked the rock walls for the quartz and gold. I moved the horses slowly, trying as always to make as little noise as possible. There was only the occasional muffled hoof beat and the creak of the saddle. I rounded a corner in the trail, scanning around me and checking the path ahead of me. Suddenly my eyes caught something I'd not seen before and I reined Archie in abruptly. I dismounted, keeping the reins in one hand, moving forward and kneeling while I studied the ground. I hadn't imagined it—there were the tracks of three or four unshod ponies. I stayed still, looking around, afraid that any movement might bring an arrow my way. I heard and saw nothing.

Finally, I stood and went back to Archie with a few quick, crouching steps. I mounted and turned both horses around, heading back for the cave. Clearly the Apaches had come this way in the last two days, because I'd seen nothing before stopping to process the gold. Lucky for me I'd chosen to stop and process when I did, but I still had to get out of here intact. The decision was easy now. I glanced at the sky as I arrived back at the cave. There was still enough light to get packed up and get a start away from here.

Kate knelt at the corner of the porch, glancing at her father once in a while, over at the other corner of the porch. Sam knelt behind the woodpile in front of her to the left, and Mike was behind the other to her right, not giving away his presence yet, according to the plan they'd made. They had come shortly after daybreak. Jim had insisted on taking the final watch of the night, and they'd all been awakened by his shot when he saw them running to take up a position behind the bunkhouse. She, Sam, and Mike had all jumped to their feet, grabbed the rifles they had near the door, and scattered to their agreed positions. She and her father had laid down a covering fire while Sam took a position behind the forward woodpile. Mike had gone out the front door and slipped, hopefully unnoticed, behind the second woodpile. They would almost certainly know there was three guns facing them, but hopefully didn't know about the fourth.

Sam hunched behind the woodpile fortress they had built a couple of weeks ago, working on the opposite question. How many guns were they facing? Based on the number and direction of the shots they'd received, he was guessing four. Someone was fairly well sheltered against the west-facing wall of the bunkhouse, loosing an occasional shot toward Jim's corner of the porch, but staying pretty well covered. One or two more were at the back side of the eastern wall of the bunkhouse, also staying under cover, only showing themselves once in a while to take a shot toward Kate's position. Someone else was working through the trees on his left, trying to flank his position. That was the one he decided to do something about. And guessing by the occasional glimpse he was catching of red hair, Sam was pretty sure who it was.

Red was getting uncomfortably close to flanking him on the left. He would also be able to get a pretty good shot at Jim's position if he got much farther. Sam turned slightly and glanced back at the others. Occasional searching fire from Red's position was making it more and more uncomfortable for him, and he was pinned by fire from whoever was on the west side of the bunkhouse whenever he tried to return fire. Red had positioned himself with a tree between his position and Jim, so he was pretty much able to fire at will. It was time for that to change, Sam thought. He hoped the others could see him clearly enough and remembered the prearranged signal.

Staying hunched behind the woodpile, Sam removed his hat and settled it back on his head. Jim and Kate immediately laid down a covering fire at the bunkhouse positions, and Mike exposed his position for the first time by levering three quick shots at Red's position. Red jerked and moved farther behind the tree, exposing his position to Sam for the first time. Covered by the fire from the porch, Sam snapped off a quick shot at Red as he came around the tree. The bullet caught him on the arm and spun him out into the open. Sam's second shot dropped him where he stood. Ironic, he thought—Red had been killed with his own gun. Some just didn't learn until it was too late.

Moving to the edge of the woodpile while he still had fire to cover him, Sam leaned out and snapped a shot at whoever was on the west side of the bunkhouse. Mike laid down several shots at the ones on the east side. Sam thought he heard a yelp back there after his second shot. Possibly just a flesh wound, he thought, but they were down a man with a possible injury to a second man, and their positions were more exposed than before. Sam stopped firing and dropped back down to the cover of the woodpile. Mike dropped down as before behind the woodpile on the right. There was total silence in contrast to the flurry of shots just a moment ago.

Nobody moved for quite some time. Sam felt pretty sure they had pulled out to think things over or to regroup, but risking his neck by standing up was not a good idea. Jim and Kate had a better view from the porch, and he would rely on them. Finally, after maybe a half hour had passed, Jim pulled himself to a standing position on the porch and waved at the others. "I could see them pull back to the trees" Jim said. "They rode off maybe ten minutes ago. I guess they're gone by now." The others stood and moved cautiously back to join the Randolphs on the porch. "How many" asked Sam? "Three of them left" answered Jim. "One was a Carson brother. Not sure about the other. You killed Red." Sam nodded and sat down on the edge of the porch. He would wait for dark before he thought about burying Red. He had no intention of getting himself killed in order to do it any sooner.

Kate sat next to her father. Once in a while her gaze strayed to Red, lying near the tree at the far side of the bunkhouse. Things swirled around in her mind. She remembered how Chance had shot Yates Carson that day in the street in Cimarron. She also remembered how Red was one of those who would have left her for dead in the upper pasture. So much had happened in so little time. She wondered if Chance would be back, and what they would have to do, with or without him.

Eventually Mike cleared his throat and moved to Kate's old position at the corner of the porch. "I'll keep watch here if you want to go inside and plan things out from here" he said. The others nodded. Kate helped Jim to his feet, and Sam followed father and daughter inside to the table in the dining room. They had won this round, but none of them really thought it was over.

An hour or so later Sam came out to the porch and knelt down beside Mike's position on the porch. Both scanned the yard and lower pasture as they talked, but things seemed to have gotten quiet for the time being. "Got to ask you to head back to town tonight" Sam began. Mike glanced over and nodded. "We need some more ammo from the back room at the saloon. Grab some sleep where you can. Stay at the saloon if you feel safe. In the morning, we need you to talk to Sheriff Stanton first thing, fill him in on what's happened here. Be sure he knows it was a sneak attack from the woods. He's a little too trusting for my taste... didn't really take any action after Jim was shot..." Sam lapsed into silence. When Mike got up and went to saddle his horse, Sam slipped into his spot on the porch and continued watching the yard.

I kept Fred reined in close behind me, moving slowly to avoid noise and constantly watching my back trail. I was headed for Denver and needed to work my way east and north. Escaping notice was a lot more important than speed, of course, and I had an uneasy feeling as I rode. They hadn't found my cave, but if they came across the spot where I'd been working the cliff walls for the gold they would be watching for me. I was intently aware of any bird calls I was hearing, wondering constantly if they were real or whether they could be signals for an ambush around any corner.

As it drew on toward mid-afternoon I crossed a shallow stream cutting through the trail and pulled over to water the horses and refill my canteen. I dipped my bandana in the stream and wiped my forehead, keeping a wary eye on the cliffs ahead of me. It all felt like ambush country to me. That started my mind down a path that might be useful. If they were aware of my presence and were setting an ambush for me, where would it be? They would catch me in the open and fire from cover, that was for sure. If they couldn't take me out immediately, they would kill the horses, strand me, and take me at their leisure. I rode a little farther and began thinking about a place to make camp for the night. I had to re-cross the Sangre de Cristo pass, and I didn't want to get there before mid-morning.

I wondered if they knew I had to go back over the Sangre de Cristo pass. That one stopped me in my tracks. I reined Archie in and surveyed by back trail while I thought about that. They might not be following me at all. They may already have an ambush set up in front of me if they'd seen me start moving. I kicked Archie in the ribs lightly and started moving again. The saddle leather creaked softly and there was a muffled clip-clop sound from the horse's hooves. I thought about a couple areas I'd come through after crossing the Sangre de Cristo pass and knew they made a great site for an ambush. There were rock falls in front of the cliffs in a couple places that would give them all the cover they would need. I wondered briefly if I should take a different path to Denver, but dismissed that idea pretty much immediately. Better to deal with a path I knew for sure could get me there than to wander and possibly become lost in the mountains.

I made my decision abruptly when I came to a clearing I could use for a campsite. I would get an early start tomorrow and use as much caution as possible as I approached the pass. The one advantage I had was to stay one jump ahead of them, if that was possible. I made a light supper without fire and watched as a half-moon climbed in the sky. I could feel a growing chill in the air. It would be more passable than it had on my original trip, because the weather had warmed considerably in the few weeks I'd been mining. After a while I wrapped myself in my blankets and lay down. The warmth was comforting, and eventually I dropped off to sleep.

Morning found me huddled in my coat and working my way very slowly toward the Sangre de Cristo pass. Every bird call was an occasion for me to stop and study my surroundings. The path elevated gradually, and the snow was still visible farther up the trail. I swung around a bend and came to the first rock fall area I'd remembered from passing this way before. I stopped the horses and looked at what lay in front of me. On my side of the trail, there was a niche in the rock wall that ran fairly deeply back into the granite cliff. I thought absently that it would shelter the horses if need be. Across the trail lay several huge boulders that had come down the cliffside at some point in the past. To ride past those boulders was a death warrant if anybody with hostile intentions lay concealed behind them.

Well, it was still early. I could stop for a while to look this over and still have time to get over the pass today. I dismounted and led Archie and Fred into the niche in the rock wall. I pulled my Winchester and three boxes of ammunition from the saddlebag. I draped my canteen around my neck and eased back around the niche to study the scene in front of me. It was all very quiet, not that it meant anything. I looked around for any signs of wildlife. It would have been reassuring to see a deer feeding or any other animal moving about undisturbed, but I saw nothing. I studied the boulders across the path. As I watched, a bird flew across the path and glided down toward the boulder in the middle. Instead of landing on the boulder, he pulled up abruptly and flew away. I had a good idea what that meant.

Holding the Winchester in my right hand, I sprinted for the two large boulders in front of me. I caught a blur of movement as I dove the last few yards for the cover of the rocks. Bullets whined above my head. I squirmed along the base of the boulders to the edge, put the barrel of the Winchester around the corner and fired a couple shots in their direction, just to keep them honest.

I studied the area around me. Nothing was moving out there at the moment. I looked for any place they could be hiding, other than behind the rocks, but saw nothing else to give them cover. Far to my right, partially hidden in a small stand of trees, were three ponies. Well, at least I had a pretty good idea of how many of them I was dealing with.

I assessed my situation. Between the two boulders was a crevice I could use to shield the barrel of the Winchester. It gave me a limited view to my front and to my right. I felt pretty confident I could keep them at bay in that direction, assuming there were no more than three of them. To my left was a little more worrisome. The angle of the boulders gave me less vision to that side. It was possible they could flank me if I wasn't careful. I took a small swig of water and kept a watch to my front, and as best I could, to the left flank. Time dragged by. They didn't seem to be in a hurry. The sun rose overhead and I took off my coat. I had enough water to last me for a couple days, but I was more concerned about what would happen if I was still here when evening fell. I checked to my front one more time then crawled over to look at my left flank. Had I seen movement out there or was it my imagination?

Chapter Fourteen

I studied the ground to my left, measuring whether it offered sufficient cover for one of them to mount a surprise attack into my position. It looked possible, with a couple rocks large enough to afford cover. There was a pretty fair amount of open ground to cross from the closest rock to where I lay. If there was some covering fire from the front, a young buck looking to get a name for bravery might give it a try.

I had a pretty good supply of ammunition, but not enough to shoot without a good target. I could afford to lay down steady fire to my front just to keep them off me. I glanced briefly to my left and saw no movement. I crawled back to the center of my position and studied what lay in front of me. There were three very large boulders across the trail to my front. There was plenty of cover for three or four men behind them. On the other side of those boulders lay a craggy rock face. The boulders had no doubt at some time fallen from that wall behind them. As I studied that rock face and the boulders, an idea came to me.

The rock face behind the boulders was an uneven surface. There were overhangs and niches throughout the face, creating a lot of angles. The boulders in front were unevenly spaced on the ground in front. That area was a semi-enclosed space, roughly circular, with rock surfaces all around. I checked my ammunition for the Winchester and mentally evaluated how many rounds I would need for what I had in mind. I decided it was enough. I would rather take the offensive than to lie here and wait for them to overwhelm me. I crawled back to my left and fired one shot, the bullet glancing off the rock closest to me. Then I crawled back to the center and sighted through the niche between the boulders.

It seemed to me that the boulder out to my front and slightly left of the other two was the most exposed position for what I had in mind. There were a number of overhangs creating downward surface angles behind that boulder, and it lay slightly in front of the other two. I could only hope that one of the Apaches was behind there. I came slowly to my knees, still shielded from the positions to my right, and laid down a steady fire off the rocks and overhangs behind the boulder to my left. The whining sounds of my bullets ricocheting off the rock told me I was making it pretty uncomfortable for anybody who might be behind there. I levered the Winchester as fast as I could, and counted ten shots as I riddled the rock face in front of me. After the tenth shot an Apache broke from behind the boulder, blood streaming from his cheek and shoulder as he charged my position. I took him down with one shot, then ran to my left.

The young buck had come off the ground behind the rocks, his ululating cry ringing off the cliffs as he charged me. I shot him dead center, then levered another shot to finish him.

I turned and ran back to the center of my position, looking to my right, afraid there was another one who had reached these boulders during the melee. Movement caught my eye, and I saw the third one headed for the horses. I sighted carefully and brought him down just before he reached the horses. I couldn't have him getting away to bring back more Apaches.

I turned and leaned back against the boulder behind me, sliding down the face of it as I moved down to sit on the ground. I sat for just a moment, letting my heartbeat come back to normal. I pulled the open box of Winchester ammunition over to me and reloaded. I turned and looked through the niche, seeing no movement and hearing nothing. It was an odd silence after the intense nonstop shooting of the last couple minutes. All three of the Apaches I'd shot lay motionless.

I wondered if there had only been three. The three horses tied up in the trees made me think so, but I'd always been a careful man and the last couple hours hadn't done anything to make me feel reckless. Eventually, though, I knew there was nothing to do but to come out and check behind the other boulders. There was nothing I could think of that was likely to fool anybody who might still be over there, and I had to get moving soon if I were going to get to safety.

I came out to my left, holding low and sprinting to the smaller rocks to my left. There was no one behind them. The one I'd shot lay in front of the closest rock, and there was no point in checking to see if he was dead. My second shot had hit him squarely in the forehead. I circled around to get a view of the larger boulders which had shielded the other two and saw that there was no one there. The first Apache I'd shot after setting up the ricochet fire wouldn't be going anywhere. I moved over to the third one, lying in front of the horses. I confirmed that he was dead also, then checked the horses. They had a small amount of food and water, which I took. I came back to the boulders and saw that they'd had three old rifles between them. I broke them over the rocks and threw them behind the bushes lining the trail.

Finally I was ready to move. I went back to where I'd left Archie and Fred and tossed the leather water pouches over Fred. The small amount of dried meat I'd taken from the Apache horses I stuffed into my saddlebags, and then mounted up on Archie. It was time to get on down the road to Denver and see if I could find Tim in his new mining supply store.

Sheriff Stanton watched as Mike mounted up outside the office and headed back down the trail toward the Randolph ranch. He sat down heavily in his office chair and stared at the wall as he considered his options. He could no longer ignore the activity of the Carson brothers, that much was obvious. He had hoped to keep trouble away from Cimarron and the surrounding ranches by just moving the troublemakers on down the road, but that wasn't an option any more. He considered where he might get some help before going out to see the Carson brothers. His instincts told him that if he showed up with armed deputies it would immediately turn into a shooting war. Was it too late to avoid that?

He considered the words of warning that old Sam had conveyed to him through Mike. Sam had advised him not to trust them at all and that there was no chance they would let him take them prisoner or allow him to move them out of the area. That went against the grain. Up until now he had been able to keep the peace without gunfire. Maybe it was time to think about hanging up the badge and moving on... eventually he came to his decision, and left the office, locking the door behind him.

Jack Carson sat in the living room of the ranch house and glared at his brother Carson and at Santos. They sat preoccupied with their whiskey glasses, not interested in stirring up Jack's famous temper any further. "How many were there?" Jack demanded. "Three or four?" Caleb glanced up briefly and shrugged. "I'm guessing four. There was gunfire from a couple places on the porch and from the woodpile in front of the bunkhouse. Mebbe some fire from another woodpile farther over." He avoided his brother's eyes and concentrated on his whiskey glass again. Santos said nothing as he adjusted the bandage around his right arm. He was in a foul mood himself, but he also avoided eye contact.

Jack got up and circled the room angrily. "So, we thought we had four against a wounded old man, a girl, and maybe an old saloon keeper." He kicked a chair out of his way and swore viciously. "And now we're down to three against four. And at least a couple of them can shoot pretty good." He dropped back into his chair and paid attention to his own drink for a while. After a while he slammed the glass back down to the table and turned his attention back to Caleb. "We still got a cousin or two over in Mora, right?"

Caleb shrugged. "We got one cousin that I know of but he might have a couple friends. He had a couple partners last I knew."

Jack stood and dug his hand into his pockets. He produced a few gold coins which he slammed onto the table, then shoved them across the table to Caleb. "Offer them fifty bucks apiece to come out here and give us some help. I don't like the numbers anymore. Tell them we might need some help getting rid of some problems. Make sure they know what we're talking about. Get back here as soon as you can." Caleb nodded, stood, and put the money in his pocket. He left without a word, saddled his horse and rode out. Jack Carson sat back down and refilled his glass.

The sheriff, acting on a whim, stopped off at the restaurant in town and went in to order a piece of pie and some coffee. He stirred the coffee absently with his spoon and looked out the window at the main street of Cimarron. The town had grown during the six years he'd been sheriff and he'd never had a situation as serious as this one. He thought again about getting some help before he went to see the Carsons. It would probably take a few days to get any help from the army, assuming they had the manpower to spare. He couldn't think of anyone in town whom he could deputize. Jim Randolph and Sam were the first two names he could think of, and they were already involved. Ironic, he thought, that the other name that came to mind was Chance Reilly. It was too late to get his help now.

He left some change on the table to pay for his food, went out and re-mounted and started down the trail to the Carson ranch. He knew it had been the O'Reilly ranch before he'd arrived in town, and there were whispers around town about how the Carsons had come to take possession. That was before his time and he preferred to let sleeping dogs lie. He drew his collar up around his neck a little more firmly as he felt a little bite from the north wind. It wouldn't be long before the leaves would start to change color, he reflected. That was his favorite time of the year.

Sherriff Stanton remained lost in his thoughts as he approached the Carson ranch. He turned through the gate and noticed that nothing seemed in good repair on the place. The gate hung loosely on its hinges and didn't appear to swing more than a foot or two in either direction. The grass was grown up in front of the house and he could see no cattle. Two horses were tied to the porch rail in front of the house. He pulled up, keeping both hands in the air where they could see clearly that he was not holding a gun. He had left his rifle back at the jail, and his pistol remained in the holster. He sat motionless for perhaps thirty seconds, hands remaining in the air as he called out to the house.

The sheriff never heard the shot that killed him. It rang out from the house through an open window. The bullet struck him squarely in the heart and he was dead before he slumped backwards off his horse and hit the ground. His horse shied away, then moved over and began cropping the overgrown grass in the yard.

Jack Carson pushed the window shut and propped his rifle against the wall near the door, where it had been until just a minute or two earlier. He watched through the window for another minute or two until he was satisfied that Stanton had come alone. He came back to the table and drained his glass, then stared at Santos, who sat across the table, saying nothing. Jack Carson reached for the bottle again, then looked over at Santos. "Bury him." Santos nodded and left the room. Carson refilled his glass.

The Sangre de Cristo pass was two days behind me as I rode down the main street in Denver. The nights had been cold, but I found I got happier with each step Archie took away from those mountains. It had been a pretty chancy thing to go up there on my own, and I know I'd had more than my share of luck. I'd found those two partly refined balls of gold left behind by someone else, and I'd found a good site and made another ball and a half or so of my own. And most importantly, I'd come away with my hair. That was the best part.

I'd had my eyes open for a mining supply store as I rode up the Denver main street, but it was a busy town and I decided I needed to ask if there was a new mining store around. It occurred to me that I didn't know Tim's last name. I swung Archie over to a railing in front of a general store when a sign on the side street caught my eye. "Tim Mulder: Mining Supplies." I swung Archie around, keeping Fred in close behind, and tied off at the railing outside the store. I lifted my heavy saddle bags off Archie and carried them through the door.

"Hey! Chance! Still got your scalp! How'd it go?" Tim crossed the room in a couple steps and wrung my hand. He stepped back and eyed the saddle bags, his eyebrows lifted. "Any luck?" There was no one else in the store, but I still found myself glancing around before answering. Tim followed my glance around the room then motioned toward a side door. "We can go in my office if you want to talk. I'll hear the bell if anyone comes in."

We went into the office and sat down on either side of an old desk. I thumped the saddlebags down on the desk, and his eyebrows lifted again. Tim didn't make a move toward the bags so I opened them, took out one of the gold balls and handed it to him. Tim tested the weight in his hand and swung toward the light to examine it. "Nice." He set the ball down on the desk and opened the bags. He reached inside and lifted the other three out, once again testing the weights and looking at them in the light. Finally he set the last one down, leaned back in his chair and whistled. "Two more the size of the first one and another half that size. You did all this in a few weeks?"

I shook my head and had started to answer when a bell from the front door interrupted us. Tim stood and motioned at me to keep my seat. "I'll see what they want and come right back" he told me, then left, closing the door behind him. I sat in my chair and fidgeted, wondering what they were worth. I had little appetite for going back for more of them if they weren't worth what I hoped. Eventually the door opened again and Tim took his seat across the desk from me. He folded his arms across his chest and waited for me to tell him the story.

I began by explaining how I had found the cave with the first two balls of gold, and how I had eventually decided to keep them. He nodded. "Nobody left those if they were able to come back for them" he assured me. "Too much money to leave behind. Either the Apaches got them somewhere out in the mountains, or they left for some reason and couldn't find their way back. Either way, they're yours now, fair and square." I nodded and finished the story by telling him how I'd mined and processed the last one and a half balls, with a short account of my skirmish with the Apaches.

Tim studied my face while I talked, and when I was done there was a small smile on his face. "Well," he said eventually, "you've been a little busy. What do you want to do with these now?" "Sell them" was my immediate answer. "That's my nest egg for the future, and I don't feel like lugging these things around. Can you put me in touch with someone?" He nodded absently. "I can." He seemed to stare at the wall behind me for a while, then cleared his throat and looked back at me.

"I can put you with someone who will buy these" he said eventually, "and I think they'll give you a fair price. The only thing might be that word will get out where it came from, and you might have to deal with people following you around and prying in to where it came from." He paused. "There's one other thing we can do, and the choice is yours." I said nothing and waited for him to continue. "I can buy these things," he said eventually. "I would pay a little less than you could probably get from someone else. But, if I buy it, no one will know where it came from and you can leave here with nobody on your trail."

I asked the obvious question: "How much would you give me for them?" Tim looked me in the eye without blinking. "$5,000. You could probably get five or six hundred more if you go through someone else. Up to you how much you want to slide by without anyone noticing all that money." It dawned on me I knew nothing about how to get paid that much money or what to do with it, so I asked that next. Tim put his feet up on the desk and leaned back. "I could give it to you in U.S. Banknotes this afternoon if you want," he said. "If you do not want the money to spend right now, that might work for you. You could open an account at the bank and put most of it in there. You might want a couple hundred in gold dollars for spending. Do you have a bank you use?"

I shook my head no. "We could walk across the street now and open an account for you at my bank—Colorado National Bank. You could have the money there this afternoon. If'n you want gold dollars, that might take a few days but we could do it. What do you say?" I thought it over for a minute while Tim went out to check on another customer. I realized that I didn't know much about banking and finance and didn't know anyone else in the entire state of Colorado, so I decided I had to trust Tim. When he came back through the door, I stood up and extended my hand. "Deal."

We crossed the street and I walked out about forty minutes later, $5,000 richer and with 100 gold coins in my bags. First I needed a place to stay, so I headed down the street with my bags and walked into Parker's Boarding House. Ma Parker was behind the desk, but I didn't think she'd remember. She looked me over as I walked up to the desk and asked for a room. "Chance Reilly?" I nodded; surprised that she had remembered me. She signed me into a room, then reached behind her and pulled out a letter. "I knew the face but wouldn't have known the name. My memory ain't that good, except this came for you a few weeks ago."

I took the letter, noticing it was written in feminine handwriting. My pulse quickened a bit as I scanned the letter and came to the name at the bottom. All thoughts of staying around to celebrate in Denver left my mind. It was from Kate.

Chapter Fifteen

Kate glanced through the kitchen window, surveying the yard and the porch. Things had been quiet for the last week, but still none of them believed this was over. Her father Jim sat in a chair at the corner of the porch, rifle by his side. He sipped a cup of coffee but his eyes never stopped travelling over the lower pasture and the trees surrounding it. A second visit from Doc Chapman had confirmed that the leg was healing. A slight limp might be par for the course from now on, but Kate knew he would never let it slow him down. Her eyes travelled to the other corner of the porch, where Sam sat with his rifle across his lap. He had been a fixture at the ranch since the day her father had been shot, and she knew they wouldn't have survived without him.

Mike had been at the ranch from time to time. They had debated whether he should return to town and keep the saloon open, but the risk was too great. The Carsons may not know that Mike had been in on the gunfire in the ranch yard, but they would probably suspect, and that would be enough for them to take action. Mike had been very valuable as it was, making an occasional trip to town for ammunition and supplies. He had been to see Sheriff Stanton to make a report on the attack last week, and was planning to return for a couple days, later on that night. Luckily there was plenty of ammunition in the storeroom at the saloon, and he was able to get food supplies at night from the grocer. They were hoping for news on the sheriff's action concerning the Carsons, if he had taken any.

Kate's thoughts returned to Chance Reilly and the letter she had sent him. She was anxious to know if he'd received the letter and if he was coming. Beyond that, though, she was worried about what he would walk into to if he simply showed up at the ranch. She had sent the letter before open hostilities had erupted. He might have no way of knowing that he could be the target in a shooting gallery. She walked over to the dining room table and sat down with a cup of coffee. She had talked to Sam a couple days ago to tell him about the cave in the hills where she had gone with Chance. She had thought this might be a way to meet up, and Chance, if he came, and might even find a way to mount a surprise counterattack on the Carsons, should they come back.

Sam had listened carefully and asked a few questions. In the end he'd pointed out that it was guesswork on when Chance would get the letter and come, and that it would also divide their forces. If another attack were to be mounted when two of them were up in the cave, it would probably be the end for whoever was left behind. Kate had agreed with the logic of what he'd pointed out. In the end though, if she felt certain that if Chance had returned to the area, she would find a way to get a message to him in the cave.

I tore my eyes from the name at the bottom of the letter and began to read:

Dear Chance,

When you left, you told me that you would absolutely come to help if I ever had need. I
never dreamed that day could come so soon, but it seems I wasn't seeing Yates or his
brothers very clearly. Things have changed so suddenly since you left.

Sam says the Carson brothers are both in town now, and he is convinced they will move against us. Sam and Dad were setting up defense positions in the ranch yard today, and we're pretty much expecting them to come any time.

Sam and his nephew Mike will help us, but we're not sure how many we are up against.
Probably Red is with them, and maybe others. We will seek help from Sheriff Stanton
but I'm sure you know he is reluctant to help.

Will you come to help us? I would be so comforted by your presence, both to defend the
ranch and to be here with me.

Kate.

I felt anger rushing through me as I turned to look at Ma Parker. She took a look at my face and took a step or two back from the counter. I stopped to get a grip on myself, and then looked back at her. "Can you tell me," I said "how long ago this letter came for me?" Ma wrinkled her brow in thought and stared at the floor. "I would say," she said eventually, "about two or three weeks ago."

My heart sunk and I stood indecisively for a few moments. Ma stood there and watched me out of the corner of her eye. Finally I pushed the sign-in sheet back in her direction. "Thanks Ma," I said. "I won't be staying here this time around after all." She nodded and took the sheet back. I scooped up my Winchester and saddle bags and headed back for the door. "Good luck" I heard her call after me. I waved the hand carrying the saddle bags in the air as I headed through the door.

I stood on the sidewalk outside the boarding house and collected my thoughts. It was two days of hard riding to get back to Cimarron and I'd pushed Archie and Fred pretty hard to get here. I was going to need to sell Fred, make sure Archie was well fed and watered, then get some supplies before heading out. I headed for the livery stable, and made a mental note to make the general store my next stop. Right after food, ammunition was going to be at the top of my list.

Mike let himself in the back door at the saloon quietly. It had taken a couple days at the Randolph ranch before Sam had finally decided it was safe for him to come back into town. He'd been to the general store to get some food, and had talked to the owner and his wife. Sheriff Stanton had not been seen or heard from in nearly a week. Word had spread around town about the attack on the

Randolph ranch, and the general opinion was that the sheriff had intended to go to see the Carson brothers about it. Mike shook his head as he eased inside the back door. He had passed along Sam's words of caution about the Carsons, but the sheriff had always done things his own way. It may have cost him his life. So far, nobody in town had wanted to look for the sheriff.

Mike lit an oil lamp and placed it in the store room, pushing the door nearly closed as he moved along the shelves, taking down boxes of ammunition for the rifles, as well as the revolvers that both he and Sam carried. So far they still had plenty of ammunition. He and Sam had decided to bring most of what they had left out to the Randolph ranch. They could always transport it back in the happy event they didn't need it.

The news most disturbing to Mike was the tidbit passed along by the storekeeper about the last sighting of Caleb Carson. Word was he had been seen passing along the road south to Mora, where it was known the Carsons had a cousin and a couple of partners who weren't exactly known for conducting themselves on the sunny side of the law. If a couple new gun hands were to come, it looked very bleak for the Randolphs as well as he and Sam. Absorbed in his thoughts as he stuffed a couple boxes of cartridges in his sack, Mike suddenly froze as he heard a slight noise coming from the back door. He eased his gun from the holster and listened. He heard a slight knock from the door again. Gun in hand, he eased out of the storeroom and toward the door.

I rode down the main street in Cimarron, wondering whether or not it was a good idea. It was dark and the street was quiet, but all the same, there were a number of people I didn't want to see. Either of the remaining Carson brothers, for starters. Sheriff Stanton, for another. That being said, I needed information and I'd already seen that the saloon was closed. I'd hoped to have a word with Sam to get up to speed on some things. I wasn't careless enough to ride up to the Randolph ranch and knock on the door. There was no telling what might have happened out there. I swung Archie into the alley in back of the stores and rode up to the back door of the saloon.

As I swung down from the saddle, I thought maybe I saw a bit of light escaping under the back door. Easing my Colt into my hand, I stepped up and tried the door. It was locked. I thought about my options, then tapped on the door with my gun and stepped back, moving a little to the side. The door swung open slowly and I recognized Sam's nephew Mike, also holding a gun, partially shielded by the door. We both breathed a sigh of relief and I stepped into the saloon, holstering my gun as I came inside.

We dragged a table and a couple chairs into the storeroom so we could have some light and still have a seat. Mike broke out some whiskey and spent about 45 minutes bringing me up to speed on the things that had happened since I'd left. He finished by telling me that Sheriff Stanton had disappeared after being appraised of the situation at the Randolph's, and that Caleb Carson was thought to be bringing in more gunmen from Mora. I rolled my whiskey glass across my forehead and thought about what he'd told me.

"It seems to me," I said, "that if those three from Mora haven't arrived yet, we might be able to stop them on the road and persuade them to go back to Mora. Are you in on that?" Mike grinned slowly and nodded. "How are you fixed for weapons?" he asked. I told him I had the Colt he'd already met plus my Winchester. "I could let you have a shotgun from the back room," he told me. "That makes a mighty good persuader, don't you think?" I agreed that it did. I told him I needed some sleep, having been on the road for two days. We made plans to be up early and see if we could turn back the gunmen coming from Mora.

Morning found me stationed at a bend in the trail a few miles south of town. I chose to stay out of sight, and sat on Archie in a stand of juniper trees to the side of the trail. Mike was dismounted and had placed himself across the road seated on a rock behind a fallen tree, his rifle resting across the tree with a clear field of fire across the trail. We had arrived at daybreak and had been there for a couple hours now, with only one traveler passing by us, no doubt unaware of our presence. Archie was cropping what vegetation he could find beneath the trees, and I was beginning to wonder if this was a waste of time.

I was glancing over towards Mike's position when I sensed that Archie's head had come up and had swung toward the road in front of me. I saw a bit of dust in the air and watched as three horses and riders became visible, coming in our direction. My gaze swung back to Mike and I saw that he was tracking their movement through the scope in his rifle. As they drew closer, I could see that each was wearing a pistol and carried a rifle in a scabbard on the horses. I decided they were worth checking out, and as they drew close I picked up the reins and nudged Archie into the trail in front of them. My shotgun lay low across the saddle, but I needed to lift it only a few inches to have them covered.

"Hi boys" I said conversationally. "What brings your to Cimarron?" They stopped abruptly and took in the shotgun and the pistol on my hip. They were silent for a while, then the one on the left spoke.

"What business is it of yours?" I glanced in his direction. He wore a gun tied down at each hip and his hand rested a few inches below the right-hand gun. He wore a greasy leather vest over a yellow bandana and he nudged his horse slightly left in an effort to flank me. I raised the shotgun a few inches in his direction and he stopped. "You might say I'm a friend of the sheriff" I said, stretching the truth considerably. He stared at me and I thought he had a pair of the craziest looking eyes I had ever seen.

The one in the center spoke up. "I heard the saloonkeeper needs help and I come lookin' for work" he said. These other two are just passin' through." "That's funny" I replied. "The saloonkeeper is a personal friend of mine, he just hired his nephew and I know for a fact he's not looking for any help." Crazy Eyes leaned over in his saddle and spit on the ground. "You got a name?" "Chance Reilly" I answered and could see in his eyes that he recognized the name. "Yours?" He didn't answer. They exchanged looks and I shifted the shotgun to the center.

"I only see two barrels on that shotgun" said the one in the middle. "And I count three of us. I think maybe you got a problem." "But then there's me" called Mike from the woods. Their eyes drifted in that direction, then back to the shotgun. The one on the right and the one in the center seemed to ease back a little, but I knew one on the left was the wild card.

"Doing arithmetic was never my best thing in school" I told them. "But it seems to me that gun in the woods changes the odds. I've got one barrel apiece for two of you, and that rifle in the woods will take down the third one before he can clear leather. I think it's time for you boys to go back to Mora. You can leave your guns here with me." They sat motionless for a second. The one on the right lifted his right hand slowly in the air and began to unbuckle his gun belt with his left hand. The one in the center moved to follow suit. I had begun to think the whole thing might pass peacefully when the one on the left went for his gun. I shifted the shotgun slightly and blew him from the saddle. He fell backwards and hit the ground, one foot still caught in the stirrup. His horse bolted, dragging him on the ground for about 15 yards before stopping. I swung the shotgun back to cover the other two, and they both lifted their hands in the air.

"Guns on the ground" I told them. "Pistols and rifles. Do the same for your friend over there. Then tie him on his saddle and take him with you." I indicated the one on the ground with a nod of my head. They complied wordlessly. When all the guns were piled in the center of the road, they remounted. One of them took the reins of the dead man's horse and they turned to go. Looking back over his shoulder, he pointed to the dead man. "That was Bud Carson you just killed" he told me. "He's got two cousins who will stretch your hide." "Thanks for the tip" I said. "Get going." They left without another word and disappeared down the trail to Mora.

Mike emerged from the woods, holding the reins and leading his horse out to the trail. His gaze followed the two remaining Mora gunfighters. "You got that right about the odds" he said. "They just got a lot better for us." I gave him the shotgun and he stowed it in his gear and swung aboard his horse. "What do you plan on next?" he asked. I thought for a second, remembering the cave where I had taken Kate when she'd been injured. "They don't know I'm back" I observed. "I wouldn't mind taking them by surprise if they storm the house again." I told him about the cave in the hills. "Kate will know where it is" I said. "I'm going up there tonight, and then I'm going to find the Carsons that are still out there." We rode back through Cimarron, then parted ways as Mike rode back to the Randolph ranch and I headed for the cave.

Jack Carson looked through the window for the fourth time in the last hour. Shadows were lengthening across the yard as the sun set. He swung around to look at his brother. "When were they going to get here?" he demanded. Caleb Carson, tired of answering the question, shrugged his shoulders. "Today. They were supposed to get here today." Santos said nothing, shifting slightly to ease the pain in his arm. For a flesh wound, it was still painful.

Jack paced back and forth across the room, cursing under his breath and stopping every few trips to look out the window again. Finally he came to a decision. Tomorrow had to be the day. He was tired of waiting.

Chapter Sixteen

Mike rode the trail back to the Randolph ranch, forcing himself to remain alert and pausing frequently to listen to the night sounds around him. He had made the trip many times now and felt pretty sure the Carsons remained holed up at their ranch each night, but he never allowed himself to become careless. When he reached the ranch, he stopped to call out the pre-arranged password for the benefit of Sam, whom he knew would be watching on the porch for the first shift that night. After caring for his horse, he entered the house and sat down in the welcome warmth of the kitchen, stacking a few boxes of ammunition on the table.

Jim and Kate gathered around him, waiting for Sam to check in from the porch. Eventually Sam closed the back door behind him and sat at the table. "Any news?" he asked. Mike grinned slightly. "I'd say news is an understatement." He recounted, to their amazement, the story of the return of Chance Reilly, the death of Bud Carson, and how two other gunfighters had been sent back to Mora. He could see hope returning to the eyes of the Randolphs, father and daughter. Sam sat back and smiled at Kate. "I told you he'd come back" said Sam, "and it looks like he made it just in time." Kate smiled back, nodded, and wiped a couple tears from the corner of her eye. "So you did, Sam, so you did." She looked across at Mike. "Where is Chance now?" Mike shrugged slightly. "He said he was going to find the other Carsons. He said something about a cave and said you knew about it."

Jim Randolph looked at his daughter quizzically. Kate sat up, the realization dawning in her eyes. "After I was thrown from my horse in the storm" she told him. "Chance took me there and cared for me while we waited out the storm." Jim nodded, watching her carefully. Kate sat back and stared at the table, a plan beginning to form in her mind. Sam hadn't wanted to divide forces before, but things seemed to be better than even in their favor, for the first time. She wanted to find Chance.

Kate looked up from the table to find all eyes on her. "I want to go to the cave in the morning" she said. Her father started to shake his head no, but Kate grabbed his hand. "Hear me out, please, Dad. If someone will go with me to the high pasture, we can follow the cliffs on the west side clear up to the stream and the tree line on the north. I can make my way across to the cave without being seen. The Carsons are to our east and they've never been over on the west side. Chance will be up there by himself against three of them if they find him up there. I know I can get there." Her gaze swung to Sam. "Sam? Just go with me to the top of the high pasture. That's all I need." Sam's eyes remained on the table. "I'm going to let your dad answer for me on this one." Kate's eyes went back to her father. "Dad. I have to go help him. Look at what he's done for us." Slowly, reluctantly, Jim Randolph nodded his head.

I waited until it was pitch dark outside before I started for the old ranch. The moon was just a sliver in the sky, which is what I was counting on for concealment. I struck the trail north of town, moving Archie along at an easy pace. I thought that probably the Carson brothers and their gunslinger friend were too confident to post a guard, knowing that the Randolphs and Sam wouldn't attack them at night. I didn't plan to do that either. I just planned to reconnoiter a little and get up to the cave. I wondered briefly if it might have been discovered since I'd last been here, but thought that unlikely.

When the trail brought me to the turnoff to our ranch—I would never be able to think of it as the Carson ranch—I dismounted Archie and walked him slowly toward the ranch yard and stable. I took off my bandana and covered Archie's nose so he wouldn't awaken anybody by snorting at the other horses. If they reacted to us, I couldn't help that. My guess was they would be too sure of their own position to get up and investigate. I moved ever so slowly through the yard and paused to count the horses in the corral. I saw only three, which tallied with what Mike had said about how many people I was facing. I saw no lights in the house. After walking Archie a hundred yards or so past the house, I remounted and continued up to the cave.

It looked undisturbed inside the cave since the last time I had been there. I tied up Archie outside, went in and lit a small fire, then leaned back against the cave wall. I was more tired than I had realized. I reached out my hands to warm them near the fire, and then reached in my saddle bag for a little food. I glanced around, smiling a little as I remembered the last time I had been here, with Kate. By now, Mike would have told her I'd come back. I couldn't wait to see her.

I began to try to form a plan in my mind for tomorrow. I needed to meet up with them only one at a time, and I knew that could be a problem. If I found all three of them travelling together, I would have to wait my chance to split one out of the herd, so to speak. Taking on two of them at once didn't seem like a bargain either, but they didn't know about me yet. I would have to find a way to let surprise give me the edge.

Eventually the warmth of the fire and the fatigue from the last few days began to catch up to me, and I found myself nodding off against a cave wall. I found some of the old blankets I had left there and shook them out, then spread them on the hay I used as bedding. As I drifted off, my mind went back to the day I'd carried Kate out of this cave. She'd told me she could have walked, but it was more fun to be carried. I fell asleep with a little smile on my face.

Morning found Caleb Carson and Santos moving across the open field toward the Randolph property. Caleb was nursing a growing anger towards his brother, Jack, who had ordered them to head over and watch the Randolph ranch this morning. Jack himself, he noticed, seemed to be staying out of the line of fire and giving a lot of orders lately. Santos rode silently alongside, favoring one shoulder and keeping his thoughts to himself. Caleb glanced sideways, then reined his horse to a halt. Santos reined in and gave him a questioning look. Caleb started to suggest that they retrace their steps to confront Jack, but thought better of it. He shrugged. "Let's swing out a little wider and come in from a different angle" he said. "We've come in the same way every time." Santos merely nodded, and they pushed their horses a little north, cutting a wider swath to the north before entering the Randolph ranch.

Kate rode against the timberline, working her way toward the cave where Chance had taken her after her confrontation with Red and Yates. It seemed like a very long time ago, though it had happened earlier this same summer. She felt like she had aged several years since that morning. She worked along the bank of the creek that fed the high pasture, knowing it would eventually lead her to the trail up into the cave.

Sam had been a little quiet this morning. She had sensed that he didn't think this was a good idea, but had done as promised, escorting her to the top of their property and seeing her off. She had, in return, promised him to come back to the ranch house directly if she failed to find Chance at the cave. Stopping to water her horse, she remembered Sam's admonition to be extremely cautious, so she crossed the stream to the edge of the trees, working along the extreme northern rim of the ranch. She watched for tracks. She could see the fence now, separating the Randolph ranch from the Carson ranch, and she searched the ground to her left, eventually picking up the trail that would lead her to Chance's cave.

There were fresh tracks on the trail, and she could see that the tracks lead in both directions, implying that someone had come and gone from the cave. Kate dismounted and led her horse into the thickening tree line, watching the trail and processing what she should do next. The most likely thing was that those tracks belonged to Chance's horse, since he'd told Mike he was coming to the cave. But the tracks implied that he had come and gone. Should she follow the tracks down the hill toward the ranch, or go on up and check the cave? And what if the tracks hadn't been left by Chance?

Finally she made her decision and led her horse up the trail toward the cave, moving slowly and watching her back trail as she went. The landmarks were no longer familiar in her mind, and the tracks seem to fade out as she worked her way up. Possibly Chance (or whoever it was) had stopped to cover his tracks at a certain point. She stopped to check another cave as she went, realizing that the landmarks were no longer fresh in her mind. The sun was beginning to work its way overhead when she finally came upon what she was looking for.

Kate tied her horse to a tree behind the cave, then worked her way noiselessly upward, watching for leaves and dead branches as she made her way forward. She paused beside the entrance, pistol in hand, listening for any noises coming from inside. She heard none. Finally she stepped into the mouth of the cave, gun pointing at various spots inside the space as she kept one wall at her back and let her eyes get accustomed to the gloom. The cave was empty. She kept the gun at her side as she explored inside. There was a bedroll on the floor, along with a few cooking utensils near a recent fire. It looked as though Chance might have spent the night.

After a search at the back, she walked forward to the entrance and pondered her next move. Chance was still by himself out there, against possibly three gunmen. She started toward her horse, but then retraced her steps into the cave. The Henry rifle lay against the back wall, with a box of ammunition nearby. She picked up both the rifle and ammunition, then headed out to her horse. She would follow Chance's trail down the hill.

Jack Carson kicked at the dying fire in the fireplace and then threw the last of his coffee on the sputtering flames. They flickered briefly and went out. He wore his perpetual scowl as he stared into the glowing embers and pondered the situation. The Randolphs, besides father and daughter, seemed to have two able guns on their side. He knew one to be the saloonkeeper Sam, whom he grudgingly acknowledged to be a salty old cuss. The other was probably his nephew. The supposed help coming from his cousin in Mora hadn't arrived yesterday, so he couldn't count on it. That meant they were outnumbered, and he never liked to be outnumbered, unless maybe he could attack from ambush.

He turned and walked out of the house, mounting up and turning his horse toward the Randolph ranch. He'd sent his brother and Santos ahead. If they used their heads, they could take up a position near the ranch house over there without getting shot. Not that he was terribly worried about it. Santos was an expendable gun. Caleb was his brother, but they'd fought from the time they were kids and Jack was ready to move on by himself. First, though, someone needed to pay for the death of his little brother Yates. Jack moved toward the Randolph property, but then changed his mind and decided to loop to the north and come in from the far side of the Randolph house. They'd never taken that route. He swung the horse in a more northerly direction and moved out.

I'd gotten a later start than I'd wanted to. The sun was beginning to climb overhead as I walked Archie down the trail, looking for any tracks other than mine and wondering how to flush the Carsons out into the open. When I reached the stream bordering the high pasture and stopped to water Archie, I got down and refilled my canteen. I knelt beside the stream, running my eye down the fence separating the two ranches. There was no movement to be seen this morning. I wondered if the Carsons had already taken up a position near the Randolph house.

I decided to work my way over toward the Carson property, staying in the trees and keeping an eye on their pasture. I knew if I climbed the hill a little I would reach a point where the fence ended and I could cross without cutting the wire. I took the reins in one hand and walked forward, leading Archie through the woods. When I reached the end of the fence line I swung around it and eased onto the Carson land. I could hear nothing other than the occasional sound of Archie's hooves scraping a rock.

Suddenly a small movement caught my eye. I peered through the trees and saw a single rider, mounted and scanning the pasture below him with binoculars. He seemed completely occupied with watching the open field below him. I tied Archie and came through the trees toward him, my right hand resting just above the holster. He saw me and started to swing his horse, but I pulled the Colt halfway from the holster and held up my left hand. "Hold it there." He stopped the horse and kept both hands in view on the horse's neck. "Get down" I told him. "Slowly."

He did as I said, but when he'd dismounted, movement on my left caught my eye and another man stepped out from the trees, a small smile on his face. Too late, I realized they had seen me first and set a trap. I reproached myself in my mind for not seeing it sooner. Too late now. The one on the right took a couple paces forward. "I'm Caleb Carson" he said. "You're trespassing on my land. We might just have to do something about that. Who are you?"

I glanced over at the one on my left. He was holding his ground so far. I swung back to concentrate on the other one. His name was Carson, which meant he was my priority. "Chance Reilly" I told him. The muscles around his eyes tightened. "Chance Reilly? You murdered my little brother." "No," I said mildly. "It was a fair fight. He had a chance to back away." His eyes hardened and his right hand moved almost imperceptibly toward his gun. The one on my left began to move slightly farther to the left. I would be impossibly flanked within a few seconds.

I knew that I was a dead man if either of them was worth his salt in a gun fight, but that didn't seem to matter so much now. I would take out Caleb Carson. I concentrated on him, aware that Santos, on my left, was continuing to move. I had to draw now... suddenly the unmistakable roar of the Henry rifle shattered the quiet of the morning. From the corner of my eye I could see that Santos had been driven backward and lifted slightly from the ground by the force of the shot. His body turned a half circle in the air before landing heavily on its left side.

Caleb Carson recovered slightly faster than me and his gun was clearing the holster a split second before mine. He fired... too soon. The angry whine of the bullet sped past my right ear and I steadied down and shot him dead center. His second shot went off uselessly into the ground. I took a half step to my left and shot again, then took another step forward and shot the third time. All three shots found their mark in his chest, and he lay still on his back as I took the last few steps in his direction. A quick check told me that both Caleb Carson and Santos were dead.

I holstered my Colt and turned when it dawned on me that someone had fired a Henry rifle and killed Santos. My hand dropped toward the holster, then moved away. Whoever it was, they were a friend. I remained rooted where I was, staring at the dead bodies, trying to absorb what had just happened. The brush on my left rustled slightly, and Kate burst out of the woods. "Chance!" I stared dumbly, trying to understand what had just happened. Kate took three quick steps and launched herself into my arms. We clung to each other and swayed back and forth for a very long time. She tilted her head back, pulled my face down to her and kissed me.

Finally I found my voice. "What…" Apparently I had found my voice but still couldn't put a sentence together. Kate laughed and filled me in quickly. "Mike came back last night and told us what happened on the road between Mora and Cimarron. I knew you would be out here against three of them, so I came to find you this morning." My eyes strayed over toward the body of Santos. "And got here just in time" I said. I glanced at the Henry rifle, which now lay on the ground at our feet. "I went to the cave first" she said. "I brought the Henry with me just in case."

I stared over Kate's shoulder. Something was nagging me at the back of my mind, but my brain was slow to respond. We were still entwined together, so I was in no mood to move either. Finally it came to mind what was troubling me. "You said three of them" I began. "Does that mean…?" Kate nodded. "I think Jack Carson is still out here somewhere." That one brought me back to reality. I bent and picked up the Henry. Kate took my hand and led me through the woods to where she had tied her horse. I saw that Archie was standing nearby. I put the Henry in the scabbard on her saddle and took both her hands. "I'm going to take the fight to him now" I told her. "I will go back up past the cave and sweep our old ranch to see if I can find him over there. If not, I'll come to your house. Please don't stay out here. Please go back to your house. I wouldn't put anything past him." She hesitated for a long time, and then finally nodded. She pulled me back down for another kiss, then went and mounted her horse. "I'll go with you as far as the stream" she said, then "I can work my way back home without being seen. I'll go the way I came this morning." I turned and mounted Archie, and we started toward the stream.

Jack Carson was riding across the tree line at the edge of his land when he heard the heavy roar of a rifle, followed by pistol fire. He reined in and listened. He counted four pistol shots besides the rifle fire. He stopped to consider what this meant. The saloon keeper and his nephew could have come looking for them. Or they may have found some reinforcements to carry the fight to him. He didn't like the possibilities. He turned his horse even farther to the north and began to work his way quietly into the deep wooded areas above him. He needed a hideout, or an ambush position, or both. He alternated riding and leading his horse on foot, making no noise as he watched the trees and pastures below him. Eventually he struck a small trail and noticed multiple sets of footprints. He knelt and studied the tracks. There appeared to have been two different riders who followed this small trail north to the higher ground, then returned. He squatted and stared up the trail for some time. Finally he mounted his horse and moved back into the woods, following the line of the trail from the cover of the trees and the underbrush.

Chapter Seventeen

We had parted ways by the stream. Kate had promised to return to the Randolph ranch house, going back the way she had come. I was determined to go back to our old ranch next door and find Jack Carson. It wasn't just about settling an old score. I had killed three of the Carsons now and had no desire to kill more. I just knew it wasn't going to be over until Jack Carson was gone.

I was well aware he was still out here somewhere and stayed alert as Archie picked his way up the trail, but I couldn't help wondering what my future with Kate might be. I was well enough off now to be the owner of my own place, or to partner with someone. I had wandered all my life and would dearly love to settle somewhere. Cimarron was really the only home I had known, and I didn't want to leave again.

I began to formulate my plan for the rest of the day. I would cut over to the east from the cave area and go back through the old ranch property. This time I would check the house. I knew that two of the three men I had seen there yesterday were now dead, but Jack Carson remained. If he were in the house again today, I would have to wait him out. If he wasn't there, I would work my way back to the Randolph house, looking for any sign of him along the way. If I didn't find him, my pre-arranged signal with Kate was to fire my pistol in the air twice before approaching the ranch house.

I passed by the cave and started working my way down through the woods toward our old house. I had dismounted and was leading Archie on foot, because the trail was pretty much non-existent at this point and I wasn't as familiar with it as I had been many years ago. I stopped for a breather and a little water for myself and Archie. As I returned the canteen to the saddle, I checked my ammunition belt and realized I was a little low. Probably there was plenty, I thought, but I didn't know for sure what the next couple days held. I decided to go back to the cave to pick up a little more ammunition before I got any farther. I turned Archie around and headed back up the mountain.

Jack Carson slipped inside the entrance to the cave, gun out and ready. He held himself against the inside wall and let his eyes get accustomed to the darkness, listening for any sounds. When he had satisfied himself the cave was empty, he returned his gun to the holster and began to explore the interior. It was clear someone had been here recently, probably last night because there was still some warmth to the fire ashes. Bedding lay tossed aside against one wall, and there was still a little food in the cave. He explored further, finding ammunition for a Colt pistol and a Henry rifle, though he didn't find the guns themselves. He squatted on his heels against the far wall and gave it some thought.

The first question, he decided, was who could possibly know about this place? Neither he nor his brothers had known about it. One piece of the bedding that lay unused at the back of the cave seemed very old, the fabric rotting away in places. So it had to be either someone who had just recently discovered an old hideout or someone who had known about it for a long time and recently returned to it. He was betting on the latter. He thought about the father and son who had lived at the ranch. He and his brothers had surprised the old man and thrown him off the cliff before claiming the ranch. The son had been sent back east, but word was that he had returned and killed Yates several weeks ago. What was the name? O'Reilly or Reilly or something like that.

Carson returned to the mouth of the cave and listened to the stillness outside. He had lived this long by not taking any chances and by getting into fights only when he had a sure thing. If O'Reilly had thrown in with the Randolphs and the town barkeep, odds were getting too long for him, especially if his brother and Santos didn't turn up. It might be time to head out. On the other hand, this could make a pretty good hideout for a few days until things settled down. And if O'Reilly or Reilly or whatever his name was should show up back here at his hideout, he could arrange a nice surprise. He turned and went back inside.

Kate rode alongside the stream at the top of the property, riding quietly and easily as she made her way back to the ranch. She and Chance had parted about twenty minutes before, when Chance went back to look for signs of Jack Carson at his old ranch. She had stopped to water her horse and to splash some cold water on her face before heading out. She had killed a man this morning, something she hadn't thought she would ever do, but there were no regrets. Santos would have surely killed Chance if she hadn't come upon them and fired. Now she just wanted this to be over, and for life to return to normal, whatever normal would be after this. She felt sure Chance would remain here and she found herself looking forward to that very much.

She found herself thinking about her mother, as she often still did. She had been a long time coming to an inner peace with the memory of her mother. She had left the ranch one day and never returned, leaving Kate and her father to make it without her. As Kate had grown older, she better understood how hard life could be here. Her mother had probably wanted a more social life in a city somewhere. Kate wondered what her mother would think of Chance. Her hand strayed to her neck, where she wore her mother's scarf. It was one of the very few keepsakes she still had. She touched her neck and reined in abruptly. The scarf was gone! She sat for a moment and thought back. She had dipped it in the stream and splashed her face with the cold water. She must have left it there. She turned the horse and started back to retrieve the scarf.

It was a matter of only a few minute's ride to get back to where she had stopped earlier. Her eyes were on the ground searching, and she saw a splash of color where the scarf had caught in some brush at the water's edge. She heaved a sigh of relief, dismounted, and retrieved the scarf. It was a sign of how disoriented she was this morning that she had ever left it there. She turned to mount and go back to the ranch when something caught her eye in the brush, up at the edge of the trail. Were those tracks? She walked her horse over to the brush and trees at the edge of the faint trail leading up to the cave. There was a set of tracks there, back in the underbrush where it would be hard to see. She followed it a few steps farther. No doubt about it, someone besides either herself or Chance had gone up there. She gasped as the realization hit her. Jack Carson! As she turned and mounted her horse, she heard the gunfire.

I stepped into the cave and I knew something was wrong as soon as I stepped in. I had become too accustomed to coming into a safe place, and it hadn't occurred to me that someone could use this cave against me. I saw movement from the corner of my eye as I stepped in, and the only saving grace was that he wasn't ready either. I froze inside the entrance and he stopped in his tracks as he turned his head toward me. We stared at each other for what seemed like a very long time. He finally spoke first. "O'Reilly, right?" "Reilly" I answered. He seemed to turn fractionally toward me. "You killed my brother Yates." "And your brother Caleb" I said. "And your Cousin Bud. Santos is dead too. Time for you to ride out of here." He seemed to turn fractionally farther, and my hand edged toward the holster. I tried to remember what Sam had told me about the brothers. Jack was the best gun hand. Make your first shot count.

I concentrated on his eyes, knowing only one of us would leave here. He dropped his eyes slightly, and then looked back up. "We killed your old man, you know." It had the desired effect. I lost concentration for just a second, and then I saw his gun coming up. I reached for mine, but first I heard the blast and felt the blow down low on my right side. I staggered backward, then steadied down and shot him. He fell back but fired again and I felt another stab of pain in my right leg. He stumbled back against a rock and began to tip over backwards. I stepped forward on my left leg and fired a shot that went in under the point of his chin as he was falling. He collapsed against the back wall of the cave.

I stepped slightly forward and to my left, dragging the right leg behind me. I fired, then stepped and dragged the leg again. Tears of rage rolled down my cheeks as I triggered the Colt again and again and again. Finally my brain registered the sound of the hammer falling on an empty chamber. I found myself standing over Carson, weaving slightly and staring down. I could see now that the second shot had finished him. I felt dizzy and weak. I moved to put my gun back in the holster, but fell to my knees instead. The gun clattered loudly onto the floor of the cave. I thought I heard Kate calling me. Was that possible? I opened my mouth to answer, but no words came. Then the blackness closed in and I felt myself pitching forward.

Chapter Eighteen

I opened my eyes slowly and the room seemed to swim around me.
I blinked twice and gradually began to bring things into focus.
Nothing seemed familiar. I was lying in a bed, but it wasn't mine
and it didn't remind me of anyplace I had been. Come to think of it,
I hadn't actually slept in a bed in a very long time. There were
windows with curtains, and flowers in a pot on the dresser.
Something stirred to my left, so I swung my eyes over there and
tried another focus. It was a woman, getting up from the chair!
Recognition came in a rush and I saw her smile. "Chance! You're
awake!" Kate leaned down and gave me a kiss.

I felt a smile spreading across my face. Kate pulled a chair to the
side of the bed and sat down, stroking my hand. I started to turn
towards her, but the pain in my side and my leg stopped me. She
put out a restraining hand. "Doc says you're to get a lot of rest and
don't try moving around much for a couple days. He said you'll

mend in a couple weeks though. I'm going to take care of you until you're better." I relaxed and lay back on the pillows. That same silly smile stayed on my face. "You can take care of me after I'm better, too" I said. She laughed and took my hand again. "Deal" she said.

I tried to remember what had happened. I knew I had killed Jack Carson, and I remembered falling forward in the cave. I asked how I came to be here. Kate explained that she had seen Carson's tracks and had come back up to the cave. When she had gone in, Carson was dead and I was lying on the floor, passed out, but breathing and with a strong pulse. She had taken a pan down to the stream, filled it with cold water and bathed my face and hands until I'd come around enough to stand with help. She'd found some rags in the cave and used them as bandages to slow the bleeding, and I'd been able to lean on her and drag myself out of the cave. She'd brought Archie around, and I'd been able to mount, with a lot of help. I had promptly passed out after mounting. She had then tied me in the saddle and brought me back to the ranch.

I absorbed that information, looking at Kate's face, a little afraid to ask the next question. I gingerly touched my side. "What about the bullet wounds?" I asked. "Will I...?" Kate smiled. Doc says you're going to be fine. You lost a lot of blood from the wound in your side, but it passed through and didn't hit any organs. Your leg will be sore for a while, but it isn't broken. Doc says you will heal up completely if you get some rest and good care. I'm going to take care of both those things." I heaved a sigh of relief and looked back up at the ceiling, knowing full well how lucky I was on all counts. Another random thought struck me: "How long have I been here?" She pulled open a curtain and let the morning sunlight stream in. "You've been here a full day" she said. "I brought you in yesterday morning."

There was a tap at the door and Jim Randolph stuck his nose in. He glanced from one of us to the other. "Can I interrupt this party long enough to have a couple words with Chance?" he asked. "Sure" I said. Kate rose from her chair. "Do I need to leave?" she asked. "No" answered Jim. "I'd like you to hear this too." He pulled a chair up to the other side of the bed and sat down. He walked with a slight limp but he looked strong.

He examined his hands for a minute before beginning. "Chance, I've been thinking – and stop me if this isn't for you." He twisted the sheets in his hand for a moment. "That ranch next door rightly belongs to your family. It was taken from you, but all the Carsons are dead now, and the land is vacant. I spoke to the people at Cimarron Bank. They hold a note on the ranch for a loan the Carsons took. It's a pretty big loan -- $3,000. They said, though, that if you could pay the note, the ranch will belong to you. So I was thinking I could..." "Done" I told him. Jim stared at me blankly. "I could lend you..." he began again.

Another big smile broke out on my face. "I don't need the loan" I said, "and I definitely want the ranch. This is the only home I've ever known. You and Kate..." The words caught in my throat and I had to stop for about 30 seconds before I could go on. "Well," I said, and then I went on to tell them the story of my gold mining experience. "So," I concluded, "I have the $3,000 and some money besides to fix up the house and start a herd. I'm your new neighbor! How about that?" Jim laughed, but there was a tear in the corner of his eye too as he reached across the bed and shook my hand. "I'll help you get started with that herd as soon as you're well. Now I'm going down to talk to somebody at the bank. You get some rest." With that he left, pulling the door shut gently behind him.

Kate's eyes were shining as she sat back down and rested her head on my shoulder. "All those terrible things happened...I started to wonder what if things could ever be normal again. Now there's nothing but sunshine. Normal is going to be wonderful." I looked at the top of her head on my shoulder and turned that phrase over in my mind a few times. "Normal is going to be wonderful" I breathed. My eyelids became heavy, and I found myself drifting off to sleep.

There was a light tap at the door, and I pulled myself to a sitting position, leaning back against the pillows. "Come in" I called. Kate came in; followed by Jim and a middle-aged man I hadn't seen before, wearing a coat and a bow tie. Jim introduced the man as Bill Samuels, from Cimarron Bank. He carried a small leather briefcase. Jim pulled up a chair for the banker and another for himself, slightly farther back toward the middle of the room. Kate leaned over and felt my forehead. "No fever" she announced cheerfully. "Are you hungry?" Come to think of it, I apparently hadn't eaten in a day and told her I was very hungry. "Good sign" she said. "I'm going to make you some soup."

Kate pulled the door shut softly behind her and I looked at the banker. He opened the briefcase and pulled out a couple documents, along with a pen. Jim pulled over a table and set a bottle of ink on the table. Samuels glanced up. "Jim tells me you're interested in buying the Carson property and are willing and able to pay their debt of $3,118 to acquire full interest in the ranch. Is that right?" I looked over at Jim. He didn't waste any time. "Yes, I told Samuels. "That's correct. I have the money in an account at Colorado National Bank in Denver." Samuels nodded and laid the first document in front of me. "This is a sales contract and a promise to pay the amount in question." He handed me the pen. I read over the contract, dipped the pen in the ink and signed. He set that one aside and picked up the second. "This letter," he continued, "says that when the amount in question has been received, you will own the Carson ranch, hereafter referred to as the Reilly ranch, in full. If you agree, I will sign the document first for the bank, and then you'll sign as the buyer." I nodded, and we both signed the letter.

Samuels swept up both documents and extended his hand. "If I may say so, Mr. Reilly, all of us at the bank and I suspect all the business people in town are glad to see the ranch returned to your family." With that, Jim opened the door and he left.

I could now hear a voice out in the living room that could only be Sam. Sure enough, he flung the door open a moment later and came in, followed by Mike. They both sat and Jim went in search of another chair. Sam searched in his pocket and came up with a toothpick. "So," he said, "I hear that when you're done lollygaggin' around here, you're going to run the old homestead." I ignored the lollygagging remark. After all, it was Sam. "Sure thing" I said. "Can't wait." Kate came in, carrying some soup on a tray, which she set down on my lap, then sat on the edge of the bed. Sam hid a smile and rolled his eyes. "By the time you get out of here" he observed, "you're going to be spoiled rotten." "Count on it" said Kate. I grinned at Sam and started spooning the soup.

Sam fished in his pocket and came up with a fresh toothpick, somehow. "You're going to have to find some help" he said. "Between the two ranches, I think we're going to need one cowboy" said Kate. I liked the way she said that. Mike cleared his throat and leaned forward. "Mr. Reilly" he said. "Chance" I told him. "I'd like to work for you out here. I've always wanted to learn ranch work and be a cowboy." Sam moaned slightly and slumped in his chair. "If that's what you really want" I told him. "You're hired as of right now." Mike beamed and sat back in his chair.

Sam moaned again. "All that work I invested in his training" he announced to no one in particular. "All down the drain." "Uncle Sam" said Mike, you know I have a younger brother who wants to come out here. "Maybe you could hire him?" Sam brightened a little. "Right," he said. "Your brother Larry". "Lenny" said Mike. "Whatever," Sam responded. He thought for a second, then threw his hands in the air. "OK. Maybe I'll make a barkeep out of one of you yet."

"Now, he needs some peace and quiet to eat his lunch" Kate announced, ushering everyone out the door. I spooned a mouthful of soup and looked at the bright afternoon sunshine streaming through the window. Who would have thought a year ago that it could ever turn out so well for an orphaned Irish boy from the city? I would take back the ranch and keep it in the family. I would ask Kate to marry me. We would raise our family here in Cimarron, and I hoped I would never feel the need to draw my gun on any man ever again.

THE END

Made in the USA
Coppell, TX
05 October 2020

39282321R00094